THE FURNITURE OF JOHN HENRY BELTER AND THE ROCOCO REVIVAL

JOHN HENRY BELTER
AND THE ROCOCO REVIVAL
Cabinetmaker John Henry Belter produced fine quality furniture in his New York City workshop between 1844 and 1863. For some years all elaborately ornamented furniture in the mid-19th-century Rococo Revival style has been called "Belter furniture." Growing interest and scholarship in 19th-century American furniture has created a need to identify furniture actually made by Belter as opposed to Belter-style furniture.
The Museum of Our National Heritage has assembled the first major exhibit of John Henry Belter furniture to define more precisely his role in American furniture making and to distinguish the work of his shop from furniture made by his competitors. Most of the Belter furniture in the exhibit is from the extensive collection of Gloria and Richard Manney, with additional documented pieces from public collections.
Unless otherwise identified, all furniture in the exhibit is by John Henry Belter based on original labels or attribution by guest curator, Marvin Schwartz.
The exhibit is supported by a grant from the National Endowment for the Arts.

CONTENTS

FOREWORD

Gloria Manney

This book and the exhibition that has been organized in conjunction with it are a dream come true for me and my husband. Collecting Belter furniture over the past fifteen years has made us realize how much a reconsideration of the contribution Belter made to furniture history was needed, and to be able to assist in the project by lending our furniture to the exhibition, so as to make it available to students interested in learning more about it, has been very satisfying.

Fifteen years ago Belter furniture was defined very broadly as being just about any example of rosewood furniture in the Rococo Revival style. A few limited it to the work in which laminations were introduced to create exaggerated curves. Now we are part of a growing group of connoisseurs who feel they can distinguish between true work from the Belter shop and the work of his competitors. We are firmly convinced that John Henry Belter was the outstanding furniture maker of the nineteenth century and we have traveled tens of thousands of miles in quest of his work.

Our first acquisition gave us no insight into what was to be in store for us fifteen years later. We never thought that we were launched on a project of developing, through trial and some error, a comprehensive collection of the work of a cabinetmaker whose work has puzzled the best of curators, dealers, and collectors. It all began with a chair I found while strolling with my infant daughter, Patricia. An unusual chair in the window of an upholstery store caught my eye. It was the first laminated rosewood chair I could recall seeing. In response to my inquiry the shop owner told me it was made by John Henry Belter, a New York cabinetmaker whose furniture was the height of fashion in the 1850s. I was delighted by the curvature of the back and the beautiful carving. I put a deposit on the chair and agreed upon the future payments that would allow me to visit my new but unsure find. On one of my mother's visits I took her to see it. She said she preferred Chippendale but thought I should buy it as it appealed to me and was inexpensive. When I got the chair home, my husband said, "If secondhand furniture makes you happy, by all means keep it." Six months later he and I attended an auction where a similar "Belter" chair brought three times more than the price I had paid. My husband observed that antique furniture does not depreciate and suddenly he wanted to learn more about *our* chair, and I found my partner was ready to share furniture collecting with me. From that moment on Richard Manney became a more avid and determined collector than I. He has been willing to go to unbelievable lengths to acquire the right piece.

That first chair is now our favorite problem piece. It had elegant rococo carving and a laminated back that made the dealer's attribution to Belter logical. Now we believe that its origins are more mysterious because it looks like nothing else we have ever found, but it is clearly of mid-nineteenth-century manufacture and we think it was made in New York. It does not look like pieces attributed to Meeks. As we learned to distinguish the work of Belter, we tended to concentrate on it, but at times we have been attracted to the work of contemporaries. At this point in our collecting career we own a few examples by other cabinetmakers, which prove Belter's competitors could produce work of quality, but these works by others also confirm our prejudice that Belter's genius made what he produced much more exciting than anything that came out of other furniture shops.

Belter may be well known, but there are problems in evaluating his work and that of contemporary cabinetmakers who produced designs in the Rococo Revival style. We hope that by studying our collection some of these problems will be solved or, at least, better understood. We agree with the men working on this monograph that breakthroughs are about to be made in distinguishing and identifying the work of the cabinetmakers who, for now, can be identified only as competitors of Belter. In the study that follows, two scientists, Edward Stanek and Douglas True, have analyzed the construction of every piece in the collection. They have compared them to at least a thousand other examples they have examined in order to outline the Belter techniques and to differentiate them from those of other furniture manufacturers. We believe that they have provided the basis for the further research that will be possible when other work is positively associated with specific makers. Marvin D. Schwartz has outlined the sources and the character of the design to distinguish the Belter pieces from those of the other makers, and, as we had hoped, the efforts expended on both aspects of the furniture confirm the theory that the finest construction and the best design occur consistently on one group of examples of Rococo Revival furniture. These all can be proven to be by our hero, John Henry Belter.

We were flattered to be asked to cooperate on this project and are thankful to Dr. Clement Silvestro, Director of the Museum of Our National Heritage, for his grace and skill in coordinating and administering a project that shows one aspect of the American genius.

INTRODUCTION

Marvin D. Schwartz

In fifteen years Gloria and Richard Manney have formed an unusually comprehensive collection of furniture by John Henry Belter. As Mrs. Manney has explained in the foreword, it all began with the purchase of a chair she no longer attributes to Belter, and the problem presented by that chair made the Manneys realize there is a need for a serious examination of mid-nineteenth-century cabinetmaking. By lending their furniture to the exhibition organized by the Museum of Our National Heritage and by providing key pieces in this study of Belter's work, they have made it possible to investigate Belter's contribution to nineteenth-century furniture making. The National Endowment for the Arts provided funding to facilitate the project.

John Henry Belter was the outstanding figure in the history of nineteenth-century American furniture. First of all, because of its fine ornament and graceful lines, Belter's furniture is a joy to collectors like the Manneys. For the furniture historian it is a phenomenon of great significance. Belter worked at the moment when the Industrial Revolution was affecting furniture production, and in the course of his career Belter changed from being a cabinetmaker to a furniture manufacturer, a fact that raises important questions.

Belter's name is associated with the finest examples of Rococo Revival furniture. He is known particularly for the work he did in laminated wood, and only recently has it been confirmed that he was not the only furniture maker to use laminated wood. Also significant is the fact that not everything Belter produced was made of laminated wood, so that this book attempts to place his work in context by seeing it as elegantly conceived and beautifully made, whether traditional or innovative in construction.

Examples by Belter in the Manney Collection illustrate the broad scope of his work. Although everything documented is in the Rococo Revival style, examples range from the relatively simple to the very ornate. Rosewood is favored most of the time, but there are pieces in oak and mahogany as well. Not easily explained is the striking consistency in the varied body of work that Belter made; because, whether plain or ornate, furniture from the Belter shop is imbued with an elegance that differentiates it from the work of other shops of the period.

This elegance is the result of the special attention to detail that is apparent in Belter's work. The laminations are thinner and the curves more emphatic in pieces by Belter. To most furniture designers the Rococo Revival style was based very specifically on the use of eighteenth-century prototypes subtly adapted to suit nineteenth-century tastes. Belter was aware of the differences between the taste of the eighteenth century and that of the nineteenth century, and he saw that the simplified flowers and shells popular in the eighteenth century were too weak for the nineteenth century. He introduced more complex ornament in the form of flowers, fruits, and vegetables that recall the style of the late seventeenth century, the period of Louis XIV. His competitors tended to update the eighteenth-century motifs by rendering them in higher relief, sometimes more realistically.

John Henry Belter's flamboyant furniture designs captured the spirit of the Rococo Revival style perfectly. They reflected the same emphatic approach to decoration that make the carpeting, the wallpaper, and the porcelain of the revival brighter than the eighteenth-century prototypes. Carpet patterns were bold, the motifs, rendered large and precisely, were colored more strongly than earlier examples. Floral bouquets on wallpapers were richly polychromed and more realistic than anything made a century earlier. In porcelain the finest examples, like those made at Coalbrookdale in England, have the same bright, strong colors used for backgrounds, and the flowers are rendered with petals that look almost real. Belter's efforts relate to the best of the Rococo Revival style, and they stand out because Belter flourished when fashionable design was in demand for decorative objects at every price level, and many manufacturers introduced compromises in quality to satisfy those who would not pay for the best.

JOHN HENRY BELTER HIS REPUTATION THROUGH THE YEARS

Marvin D. Schwartz

John Henry Belter (1804–1863) stands out as the most famous cabinetmaker of the Rococo Revival era, but distinguishing his work has been challenging. A New York craftsman whose shop was first listed in directories in 1844, Belter, according to the listings, operated first as a cabinetmaker and then as a furniture manufacturer until his death. The firm continued to do business until 1867. As far as is known, Rococo Revival furniture was all that Belter produced, although all evidence shows that his contemporaries followed the trends of the period and worked in a variety of styles. From surviving marked pieces we learn that two of the best known, J. and J. W. Meeks and Alexander Roux, made Elizabethan, Gothic, and Renaissance revival furniture as well as a modified version of the Empire style in the period between 1840 and 1870. Because Belter's name has commonly been used as the generic term for all Rococo Revival furniture but particularly for examples made of laminated wood, it has taken some effort to differentiate the work of Belter from laminated-wood furniture made by others. Almost any reference to *Belter* furniture in articles written before 1965 involved the generic use of the term.

In considering the question of furniture production in the middle of the nineteenth century it is important for researchers to remember that documenting furniture-making activity in 1850 New York is as difficult as documenting that activity in ancient Rome. The names of over 400 cabinetmakers are listed in Doggett's *New York City Directory* for 1851–1852, but what each of them did is not easy to learn. Some of the men listed may have been in the employ of others, and others operated large shops employing huge staffs, but there are few records to suggest the key manufacturers. Even though Belter was listed, there is no indication of his significance. Although Belter was the single New York craftsman to obtain a series of patents as early as he did, no articles in newspapers or magazines have turned up with references to his accomplishments. The scholar has only the patents themselves to consider. They reveal an innovative approach while disclaiming the use of the laminating process itself as being new and patentable.

One would assume that if Belter was famous in 1853 he would have been mentioned in the popular pictorial account of the New York Crystal Palace exhibition, *The World of Science, Art and Industry,* by Benjamin Silliman and Charles Rush Goodrich (New York: G.P. Putnam & Co., 1854). Curiously enough, the authors ignored him although they mentioned Roux, Herter, Hobe, and a number of other furniture makers. Although not in the illustrated account of the event, Belter's exhibit piece is listed in the offical catalogue (which was a simple listing of the objects without pictures) as "Round Centre Table of ebony and ivory." Recently discovered, only half of this important table was acquired by the Manneys, because this piece had been sawed into two pieces just above the stretcher, and the bottom half, with a glass top, is reported to have been seen in Kentucky.

Besides the work itself, which is distinctive, substantiating Belter's importance is possible by using the few surviving records that provide evidence of his activity. First of all, the few bills that have survived show that a parlor set by Belter cost about $1,200, which means that it was expensive yet priced about the same as the work of any of the best-known, fashionable New York cabinetmakers of that time. The records of Dun and Company (now known as Dun and Bradstreet) at the Baker Library of Harvard University include comments on the financial position of many New York businesses. In the 1850s the reports were based on informal inquiries, and the company records have yearly references to Belter, which suggest he was a good risk who could be counted on to pay off any debts he might incur; but one statement made is that the quality of the furniture produced was too high for the business to be as profitable as that of some of his competitors.

That a continuing interest in Belter furniture after its manufacture had stopped is evident in early photographs of eclectic interiors. The Rococo Revival style went out of fashion in the 1860s, to be replaced first by the Renaissance Revival and then the Eastlake style and eclecticism. *Belter* furniture—mainly chairs—was used in eclectic interiors in the 1880s, and it can be seen in photographs of the period. However, the furniture shown suggests a generic use of the Belter name. Turn-of-the-century collectors who would ignore most furniture made after 1830 found the effects of Belter, or at least the work then called Belter, appealing enough to pay about the same price for it as for much earlier American furniture.

The first serious revival of interest in nineteenth-century furniture that included examples of work by Belter and his imitators came in the 1930s when both The Metropolitan Museum of Art and the Philadelphia Museum of Art held exhibitions. Curators in both museums were interested in documenting styles that were being ignored. At the Metropolitan the exhibition had surveyed New York State furniture from its beginnings, but Philadelphia had concentrated on the nineteenth century. Comments in reviews of these shows suggested that there were many who could not tolerate the extravagances of the Rococo Revival, but at the same time others were making the discovery of its appeal. At sales and in certain middle-level antiques shops Belter was attracting attention, and it was the most coveted nineteenth-century furniture. Adventuresome collectors like Juliana Force, who was to become the first director of the Whitney Museum of American Art in New York, found Belter appealing. The fabled cosmetics and perfume manufacturer, Helena Rubinstein, furnished her New York drawing room with Belter furniture displayed against paneled walls hung with modern School of Paris paintings. The question of whether the taste for Belter's work was concentrated in a few parts of the country cannot be answered as the original areas where Belter was fashionable are not easily located today. In the 1930s and later Belter furniture was considered more marketable in the South than in the North. There is evidence that many fine examples that had been used as the original furnishings of houses all over the country were shipped in recent years to Georgia, Tennessee, Louisiana, and Mississippi.

The current revival of interest began around 1960 when The Brooklyn Museum held an exhibition called "Victoriana: Exhibition of the Arts of the Victorian Era in America." The exhibition surveyed the American arts between 1830 and 1900, with the sequence of styles differentiated and discussed. The radical changes that took place in the course of the nineteenth century were emphasized to prove that there is no single Victorian style. The timeliness of the show was proven by the extensive newspaper and magazine coverage it received. Syndicated columns appearing in over 400 newspapers published all over the United States reported on the exhibition. Magazines like *Interiors,* primarily of interest to designers, illustrated examples in the exhibition, and for the first time in years designers and design critics, seeing the differences in the various styles of the Victorian era, became aware of the quality of fine Rococo Revival design. Belter furniture was taken seriously by a group of collectors who were to grow each year in both numbers and enthusiasm. Whereas in 1960 there was little growth in the popularity of "Belter furniture," by 1965 evidence of the demand was discernible. The differences between works in laminated wood were also increasingly evident. Hagen had made the point that Belter had competition, and Joseph Downs's 1948 article in The Magazine *Antiques* (54, no. 3 [September 1948], pp. 166–168) suggested that it was possible to identify laminated Rococo Revival designs by other cabinetmakers. In 1964 John N. and Lorraine W. Pearce, collaborating with Robert Smith on a series of articles in The Magazine *Antiques* on "The Meeks Family of Cabinetmakers," reported on the parlor set that Joseph Meeks's daughter and son-in-law had received as a wedding present. It was in a design that had been associated with Belter but was simpler in detail and cruder in construction, so that an attribution to Meeks was logical. Since then other attributions have been suggested for work that is not quite so elegant as the documented examples by John Henry Belter. Recently, furniture has been found in Boston and Philadelphia with evidence to suggest that the pieces were made locally. A few years earlier there would have been no question about attributing the work to Belter.

The new attributions have narrowed the conception of what the Belter shop produced to a group of related works of very high quality. Today he appears to be more of a genius and an innovator than was true when *all* laminated furniture was attributed to him.

The earliest proof of Belter's high reputation is to be read in an account written by Ernst Hagen, a cabinetmaker who began his career in New York in the 1840s. This account by Hagen is in the memoirs he wrote in 1908 in a notebook preserved in the Downs Manuscript Library of the Henry Francis du Pont Winterthur Museum (they were published in 1963 in The Magazine *Antiques*). Hagen makes reference to "Belter furniture," which shows he used it as a generic term rather than as an attribution referring to the work of a single shop, an indication that the use of the term to mean laminated furniture was part of a firmly entrenched oral tradition at the time he wrote. This would explain why such examples as the Freiberger parlor set in the collection of the Cincinnati Art Museum has been called *Belter* since it was bought in 1863. Family tradition included the story of its purchase in New York. The pattern of the ornament and the way the pieces were constructed are not like any work by Belter, but there is a strong resemblance between the Freiberger parlor set and sets that have been attributed to another shop, that of Belter's competitors, J. and J.W. Meeks.

Hagen's account is unusual because it also provides an early reference to laminated furniture. Most references to furniture in early advertisements or the catalogues of exhibitions have no mention of innovative construction but rather insist on the evidence of traditional skills like carving. Tradition appears to have been more salable than novelty. Typical for the time is the description of one of the few examples of American furniture at the London Crystal Palace exhibition of 1851 ("The Industry of All Nations"), a spring chair made by the American Chair Company, following a patent of 1846. As it was made of iron, it must have been difficult not to refer to the novelty of the piece, but the commentator finds that "The design and fittings of these chairs are equally good and elegant, and certainly we have never tested a more easy and commodious article of household furniture" (*The Art Journal Illustrated Catalogue. The Industry of All Nations* [London: George Virtue, 1851], p. 15). He makes no mention of the use of iron for an indoor chair or of the fact that a patent was obtained for the unusual spring construction. Hagen, on the other hand, does refer to Belter's unusual technique and, although there are no contemporary records of patent-infringement suits because of the significance of Belter's patent for lamination, Hagen speaks of the possibility. Hagen's recollection was fairly accurate in attributing a characteristic type of chair to Belter. However, he described a method of constructing chairbacks of laminated wood used by his employer, Charles A. Baudouine. Despite Belter's disclaimer of innovation through the use of lamination, Hagen reported that to avoid lawsuits for patent infringement, Baudouine introduced an extra seam down the back of the chair. The paper labels that Belter used bear no mention of the fact that he had obtained patents, but the stamp used on some of the beds have the date of the bed patent.

DISTINGUISHING BELTER AS A GENERIC TERM FROM BELTER AS A CABINETMAKER

Marvin D. Schwartz

The documented furniture by John Henry Belter includes the most splendid examples of the Rococo Revival style. Gracefully curving forms embellished with elaborately carved decoration were executed with amazing skills. When necessary, flamboyant shapes were made by using laminated woods, but not all Belter produced was of laminated wood, neither was it all decorated with carving. The single criterion was beauty and it was achieved through the knowing use of woods. While rosewood was favored as the most fashionable of the time, oak and mahogany were used as well.

Connoisseurship can be a very frustrating field when there is a need for new evidence to be uncovered. At this point it is obvious that work that has been referred to as Belter furniture can be classed in several separate groups reflecting differences in design and techniques of construction to suggest that there were a number of manufacturers active in the production of laminated Rococo Revival furniture. In the main the work that looks as though it is not by Belter is not easily associated with another maker. The only signed examples are the work of two Philadelphia cabinetmakers, George Henkels and Charles White, and they invite further research to prove that the names applied were of the makers and not the distributors. As we have seen, the growth of interest in Rococo Revival design since 1960 has inspired a new, more careful approach to making the attributions. This is part of a new trend toward investigating the origins of furniture made all through the nineteenth century. Graduate study in the American Decorative Arts, which began at Yale University and The Henry Francis du Pont Winterthur Museum and spread to the New York State Historical Association at Cooperstown and a number of other schools, has trained new generations of "sleuths" searching out the documentation of objects. The differences in the decoration are possibly more obvious than those in the construction. The work by Belter's competitors has simpler carving and, more often than not, elements that derive from Renaissance or neoclassical sources. Gadrooning is used as a border; classical pediments top various chair designs. They reflect another taste and, to show how much they were admired, where bills with prices have survived, the prices are as high as on Belter bills. There is also the explanation by Hagen that his former employer's "most conspicuous productions were those rosewood over decorated parlor suites with round perforated backs generally known as 'Belter furniture.' "

A major point of confusion is the consistency of the category of laminated furniture attributed to Meeks. The daughter's set is part of a large group of similar examples that have New York histories, so it would also be logical that it was the work of a large, successful manufacturer who would have been capable of producing on a relatively large scale, and the Meeks shop was certainly capable of extensive production. If only Meeks had not marked so much of its other output. One can find labeled Meeks furniture in just about every style. There are Empire, Gothic, Elizabethan, Renaissance, and even Rococo Revival examples made of solid wood that bear the stenciled mark of J. and J.W. Meeks, or an earlier variation. But no *marked* example made of laminated wood has been found. Another New York cabinetmaker, Charles Klein, also may have made laminated furniture. His family donated a chair to the Detroit Historical Museum that was closely related to work by Belter, which may well have been made by Klein, but Klein's marked furniture is much less elegant.

Laminated furniture has been attributed to the Philadelphia cabinetmaker George Henkels on the basis of a signature found on a laminated parlor set that had been offered to the Manneys several years ago. The photograph of the set suggests that it was made in a design that is a simple variation of the Rococo Revival style. In an advertisement illustrating an array of Henkels's furniture, there is a chair with a pierced-work frame around an upholstered back that might well have been laminated. It resembles a chair at the Maxwell Mansion in Germantown, outside of Philadelphia, that was marked by Charles White.

An elaborately ornamented laminated-back chair

at the Museum of Fine Arts in Boston has been proposed by Jan Seidler of the museum as the key to laminated work made in Boston. The attribution is based on the discovery of remnants of Boston newspapers on the inner side of the laminated back. This newsprint had been left on when the piece was first upholstered in the 1850s, and it was leftover paper from this protective layer that had stuck to the back after it had been bent into shape in the caul, or mold, that was used in the operation to curve the back. The use of local paper is logical, and it had to be more than a coincidence that Boston newsprint was found on the chair that had a long Boston history. Other examples that have been investigated suggest that the same patterns may have been used by Belter over a long period, because one example of a pattern was found with 1849 newsprint on its back, while another example in the same design was documented by a bill dated a decade later. Another chair that is believed to have come down in a Boston family was a gift to The Brooklyn Museum from Mrs. Charles S. Jenney. It, too, is similar to Belter in design, but the details are rendered with less elegance and the construction is not so fine as that characteristic of Belter pieces. The roses

1. Side chair, rosewood with laminated, pierced back. (*The Brooklyn Museum, Brooklyn, New York; Gift of Mrs. Charles S. Jenney*)

and grapes in the pierced-work frame are in a pattern that is different in detailing and spacing from work by Belter. The scroll feet also differ from the usual Belter examples (fig. 1).

Attribution of work that is neither labeled nor documented is a challenge that has been difficult to meet. One group of pieces, a set in the Smithsonian Institution and another in The Bayou Bend Collection, Houston, Texas, is considerably different from the work of Belter or the so-called Meeks. David Warren of The Bayou Bend Collection found a similarity between the decoration on some pieces of the Texas set and that on a sofa by Alexander Roux that was illustrated in the Silliman and Goodrich publication on the New York Crystal Palace exhibition. The arguments are valid in that the motifs on the Roux sofa known from an engraving are similar to those on the sets that are known. However, there is no work by Roux made of laminated wood that can be more definitely identified. Again, although the possibility is strong, that last piece of evidence required to make the attribution stand without question is still lacking. In the case of Roux descriptions of his work are more extensive than for other makers of his time. Andrew Jackson Downing in *The Architecture of Country Houses* (New York, 1850; reprint ed., New York: Dover Publications, 1969) mentioned how fine Roux's work was, and illustrated a number of examples from the Roux shops, but there is no hint that anything by him was laminated. Special machinery was required to produce laminated wood, and the Roux shops may not have had such equipment.

Considering the fact that there were many cabinetmakers working in New York in the 1850s, it is possible that a new document or an example examined more carefully will present evidence that will prove another of the names in the directories to be significant. It would take only one or two documented or marked examples to make a large body of examples fall into place. Although New York was very likely the source of elegant furniture, other centers kept up with its production of fashionable designs. Philadelphia and Boston may prove more important as time goes on. The Rococo Revival was significant in both cities, and there is evidence that each may well have had cabinetmakers producing furniture of laminated wood. In the West, although the industry was taking root and factory production was beginning in several centers such as Cincinnati, St. Louis, and Grand Rapids, no work as elegant as the furniture made of laminated wood has been identified. There is evidence that the new factories were responsible for inexpensive wares, but they could have had expensive lines as well, as that was to be their practice after 1870. Later in the century the Grand Rapids factories produced both plain and elaborate furniture. The difference was in the amount of labor expended. There is no evidence to prove it, but the same range of furniture may have been produced in 1850.

Although New Orleans was a significant center of the furniture trade, and there is evidence of the activity of local cabinetmakers and several New York cabinetmakers had warerooms there, no locally made laminated furniture is known. Investigations of the origins of elegant furniture from houses in the vicinity of New Orleans too often yield family histories that claim France as the source of work that is called *French Style* in design books of the mid-nineteenth century. As more is learned about local work, some furniture made of laminated wood may be identified as the work of New Orleans cabinetmakers. To date, New Orleans shops, particularly that of Prudent Mallard, have been credited with making furniture of solid wood that is as elegantly carved as the best of Belter.

There is enough of a range in the character of the carving and the design of Rococo Revival laminated furniture for it to be relatively easy to identify the work of John Henry Belter. A group of documented pieces, identified by association with bills or with labeled work, have a consistency in design, methods of construction, and ornamentation that make for a distinctiveness that is unmistakable. The work that came out of the Belter shop differs from most Rococo Revival furniture because the basic approach to design is much more complex and the techniques of construction are much more subtle. Elaborately carved furniture made or, at least, sold in New Orleans includes examples that sometimes are decorated with motifs used by Belter, but the construction is more traditional. The combination of superb construction, fine carving, and well-conceived design appears to have been unique to Belter. A question has been raised by those who would prefer to think that most laminated work was made by Belter. They believe that the two or three levels of quality could have been made in a shop with expensive and inexpensive lines. They theorize about the range of design and visualize a knowing manufacturer designing for several price categories. Although this would have been possible, the contrast in approach as it affects details is so great that it is difficult to imagine the same shop turning out the different kinds of designs. Also, there is an amazing consistency in the work that has been attributed to Belter in recent years. Even though it is still difficult to know the source of the lesser examples of laminated Rococo Revival furniture, the finest examples all appear to have been conceived by the same designer and made in the same shop. The attribution of eighteenth-century furniture of high quality to a single maker has been proven wrong because labeled examples by different makers in a single design have been discovered. However, in the case of Rococo Revival examples, the fact that special patented techniques were used means that attributions to makers based on the comparison of details and design are more logical. There is an extensive number of variations on a limited number of basic patterns, and the parlor sets that have survived intact were rarely made with the decoration exactly the same on each piece. How much the shops produced in a little over twenty years of production is a question that cannot be answered easily. Neither can the changes in production techniques that took place in the transition from John H. Belter "cabinetmaker" to John H. Belter "manufacturer" be noted. The opening of the factory, miles uptown at Third Avenue and 76th Street, is mentioned for the first time in the 1854 directory, but in the 1853 official catalogue of the New York Crystal Palace exhibition Belter is listed as a manufacturer. Probably differences between the furniture made before and after the move into the factory are not evident because the expansion was a way of increasing the work force rather than changing the techniques of furniture making. The greater number of craftsmen employed in the new factory practiced their skills much as they had done in the smaller establishment, and, as in the smaller establishment, the distinctive element was the mind of John Henry Belter. An article on George Henkels in *Godey's Lady's Book* is eloquent in describing the role of the manufacturer:

> But, in rising higher, to a style more florid and ornate where the *carver* is to decorate and embellish, it will be readily seen that the presiding mind, the master-spirit of such an establishment should be qualified, not only by good native parts, but by a natural bias, for this particular art . . . ("A Visit to Henkels' Warerooms," *Godey's Lady's Book,* 41 [August 1850], p. 123)

Belter was most certainly the guiding force at a factory that produced unusually fine work.

For the connoisseur today the work of John Henry Belter is easy to recognize and hard to explain. It is distinctive in both design and execution, an extraordinary phenomenon of the middle of the nineteenth century. Although the hints of elaborate Rococo Revival forms, characterized as *French style* or *Louis XIV,* can be found in design books as early as the 1820s, nothing quite like a Belter design is to be found in the fashionable efforts of the cabinetmakers of London, Paris, or any other Old World center. The development of the technique of bending laminated wood into curving shapes enabled Belter to create designs that were more flamboyant than anything made of solid wood. Belter's reputation is based on the parlor sets he made, and for those who have investigated his work, the beds and bureaus are also well known. As his work has been increasingly studied, it appears that the Belter shop produced hall and dining room furniture, too. Although Belter is associated with the use of laminated woods to such a degree that it is regarded as his signature, it turns out that there is significant furniture made of solid wood by Belter. Using the Manney Collection as the point of departure for defining the "Belter touch," it is possible to see his characteristic products and to develop an understanding of the excellence of the work by his competitors, who conceived designs that could be executed more quickly and less expensively but were equally rococo.

TECHNICAL OBSERVATIONS

Edward J. Stanek and Douglas K. True

The attribution of a given example of nineteenth-century furniture to the category of Rococo Revival is a talent relatively easily acquired by training the eye to recognize motifs, shapes, and materials. However, the task of specializing further to reveal the particular factory or cabinetmaker responsible for a specific piece ideally requires authenticating documentation. When such documentation is limited, a detailed knowledge of such pieces coupled with a mechanism for recognizing and quantifying similarities in style, materials, craftsmanship, and construction is also required. A review of works that can be unquestionably attributed to Belter is the appropriate starting point in developing a methodology for the examination and attribution of furniture not so well documented. Comparisons of technical details among the examples contrasted with appropriate patents can reveal facts otherwise not apparent.

LAMINATIONS

Rosewood from either Brazil or East India was the material favored by mid-nineteenth-century patrons of formal furniture. Rosewood receives its name from the faint odor of roses detected when it is scratched or cut. Although beautifully colored and figured, rosewood is very dense, and although oily, it is brittle. Chairs have been known to break under their own weight when stress was placed at particular places on chairbacks while being moved from place to place, or from a sharp blow when toppled.

Laminated woods were used to obviate this problem in complicated furniture designs. The process of laminating involved gluing together sheets of wood with the grain of adjacent sheets oriented in different directions. A sheet of wood is most apt to fracture from a stress applied along its grain and is least likely to fracture from stress applied perpendicular to the grain. By gluing together successive sheets of wood with the grain placed in different directions, a blow sufficient to break sheets of solid wood could be withstood.

A further modification is made by curving each sheet and preventing it from returning to its original shape while being glued to other sheets. John Henry Belter termed the restricting devices *cawls* or *cauls*. They were designed to press together a number of veneer sheets and to hold them in a certain form while the hot glue that was applied between the sheets cooled. The furniture resulting from such a process is thinner and thus lighter than if made of solid wood and has the same resistance to breakage.

Modern plywood is an example of laminated wood. Figure 2 shows an example of laminations in a Belter pierced-carved bed. The seams between the adjacent layers are apparent. Because the intricacy of elaborate open carving leaves many areas of wood with a very thin cross section, it is not likely that such pieces

2. Detail showing the layers of veneers on a Belter bed. (*The Brooklyn Museum, Brooklyn, New York*)

would remain intact over a long period of time without the use of laminations.

CONCLUSIONS

Conclusions that are to be derived and substantiated later in this text are as follows:

1. Although it is possible that many furniture companies and cabinetmakers produced laminated furniture, there are only two distinct groups of such furniture that comprise the bulk of surviving examples.

2. One group definitely is made by John Henry Belter. The other group is weakly associated with the firm of J. and J.W. Meeks.

3. Although unlaminated Belter furniture can be found, the name Belter is associated with laminated examples that incorporate layers of veneer averaging less than 0.063 inch (1.6 mm) thick, with the possible exception of beds, which could be made from thicker veneers.

4. The other major group of laminated furniture is made from veneers approximately twice as thick as the veneers in the Belter group.

5. Pierced-carved examples of Belter seating furniture are generally outlined by sweeping, interconnected "arabesques" and, in contrast to examples by other makers, decorative C-scrolls are rarely incorporated in any pierced-carved piece. A few C-scrolls are found on Belter tables and beds, however, most of the continuity in the openwork is maintained by naturalistic motifs such as branches, leaves, and vines. Acorns, grapes, and other fruits, nuts, and flowers were relied on very heavily.

6. Decorative C-scrolls are the prevalent linking mechanism for the carving on thickly laminated openwork by Belter's competitors. Grapes, other fruits, and flowers were also favored motifs.

7. Belter used cylindrical, conical, and spherical cauls for chairbacks.

8. Thickly laminated furniture was not made in spherical cauls.

9. Belter employed the use of applied, solid crests (as did others) for chairbacks prior to 1850 and perhaps later. These early chairs are most likely to have been executed by Belter's own hand or under his close supervision.

10. Some Belter chairs have solid, carved side rails, while others have a side rail covered with a single sheet of veneer tapered from the laminated chairback.

11. The earliest of the Belter pieces incorporated laminations throughout the thickness of an openwork chairback, and these pieces were made of mahogany. Later, solid work was applied to extend the carving relief over a base of seven or more laminations.

12. Belter produced furniture without pierced carving as well as openwork throughout most of his career.

13. The patterns of furniture produced were not done by model year as in the modern trend with American automobiles but rather executed continuously after their development, as long as the demand continued.

14. Openwork was produced by Belter prior to 1847.

15. The rear legs on Belter chairs generally have a noncircular cross section.

16. The rear legs on the family of thickly laminated chairs have a circular cross section and taper from thick near the seat to thin near the floor.

17. Most Belter chairs originally had casters on all four legs, usually brass platform casters with hollow brass rollers.

18. Most thickly laminated chairs were designed to have casters only on the front legs, usually capped brass casters with rubber, wood, or brass rollers.

19. Belter chairbacks have one or more outer seams that penetrate either one layer of veneer for chairs made in the "ordinary way," or two layers of veneer for chairs made from staves.

20. Belter laminated furniture is made with the adjacent layers of veneer having the grain at right angles to each other, except for a very thin layer occasionally placed as the outer layer for cosmetic purposes.

21. Thickly laminated furniture generally has at least two adjacent layers of internal veneer with the grain parallel.

22. Several associated patterns of Belter chairs were made from the same cauls, with progressively more complex carving added to distinguish one pattern from the next.

23. Many sets of seating furniture were made by Belter in a given pattern, with only slight variations to distinguish one set from the next. The variations occurred through the permutations of the motifs carved on the seat-rails, feet, and knees of the chairs, or by rearranging a fixed motif on the chair crest.

24. Fruits, nuts, and flowers appear on the finials mounted on the stretchers of Belter tables.

25. Fruits and nuts but not flowers appear on the finials of the family of thickly laminated tables.

26. There exists a pattern for thickly laminated tables that matches corresponding patterns of seating furniture.

27. Belter tables were not developed with patterns associated with seating furniture.

28. Belter chairbacks fit into the seat-rail in such a manner that the back envelops the rear seat-rail.

29. Thickly laminated chairs have backs that mount on top of the seat-rail.

30. Belter was an innovator, as exemplified by his

patents. Many anomalies may be found, which resulted from his experimentation and which will be difficult to attribute.

31. Belter distributed his furniture through retail outlets outside New York.

32. The simple possession of thin laminations or thick laminations is not evidence enough for attribution but must be considered with other evidence collected. The conclusions stated above for "thickly laminated" furniture do not apply to all furniture with thick laminations but rather to the specific and prolific family of furniture now loosely attributed to the J. and J.W. Meeks factory.

SEATING FURNITURE

Seating furniture is by its very nature the most difficult to find with a surviving label. The cabinetmaker would have had either to expose a signature or tag, or to affix it in an unobtrusive location. The assumption must also be made that the manufacturer found sufficient motivation for such identification. It appears obvious that in the case of laminated seating furniture no easily accessible identifying marks were affixed by furniture makers, in contrast to such identifications on many oil paintings, bronzes, and other works of art produced by painters and sculptors. The removal of upholstery materials on scores of samples has led to the conclusion that labels were not hidden in the bowels of horsehair and cotton. The most likely location for an identifying tag appears to be the underside of a seat where it remains hidden during normal display. Such tags would have to be attached with a tack to the seat-rail or affixed to the wood or cloth dust cover with an adhesive. Needless to say the ravages of time deteriorate adhesives, textiles, and papers. Exposed tags very likely would have crumbled in the past century when subjected to the flexing of a seat in use or would have been removed to allow the replacement of worn fabrics, twine, and springs.

It is easy to understand why surviving labeled examples are so rare. There exists a double parlor set of seating furniture on display in the mansion called Rosalie in Natchez, Mississippi. The set is supposed to have been purchased by the daughter of the mansion's owner in 1859 or 1860.

Fannie McMurtry Wilson was studying in New York and was asked to select suitable parlor furniture before returning home. The set has traditionally been attributed to Belter although no documentation of its origin has been recently available to add credence to the legend. In the Manney Collection are a number of examples (see plates 2, 3, 44) essentially the same in design and construction as those at Rosalie. This pattern, with laminated woods and a solid rosewood appearance on the reverse of the chairbacks, is not pierced-carved but falls into the category of examples historically thought to be Belter. An armchair in the collection of Ronald and Carol Harris is also done in the pattern of the Rosalie chairs. This design is the most common of Belter's surviving works, with examples to be found in both public and private collections nationwide. The Harris armchair has been reupholstered but a label similar to the one pictured in plate 55 has been preserved in remarkable condition glued to a fragment of the dust cover that originally protected the underside of the seat.

Markings on the label identify the maker as J. H. Belter, "Manufacturer of All Kinds of Fine Furniture." The factory address given is Third Avenue at 76th Street and the warehouse address is 552 Broadway. Since the factory was opened in 1854, as indicated by its listing in a New York City street directory, and the warehouse address was established in 1856, the chair appears to have been made after 1856. Up to the time of this writing, it would appear that the manufacturing of each pattern extended over a long period. Side chairs in the Rosalie pattern exist in another private collection with a variation in seat shape but they are essentially the same chairs as those under discussion above. Paper labels remain tacked to the underside of the seat-rails of the worn chairs still bearing the original upholstery. They read "John H. Belter, fancy cabinet maker, 372 Broadway, New York." The labels further specify "Orders promptly attended to" and they are dated in pen and ink "1852." Combining the above information, we find that Belter produced the same basic chair over a period of at least seven years. More important, this design, commonly called Rosalie, was produced by Belter during his tenure as a cabinetmaker, when furniture was made to order, and also during his tenure as a manufacturer, when his factory turned out an inventory in a quantity substantial enough to require a separate warehouse. Possibly emphasizing the significant transition that took place in a few short years was the hiring by Belter of forty apprentices in 1854, as reported by earlier scholars.

Two important sets of pierced, elaborately carved seating furniture were made for Green Hill Jordan and Benjamin Smith Jordan, two brothers who had married two sisters. The sets have remained intact through the years. One is now on display in the governor's mansion in Austin, Texas, and the other set is maintained in a private collection in Georgia. Bearing the date September 5, 1855, the original bill of sale conveying furniture from "J.H. Belter & Co. to Col. B. S. Jordan" still exists. The address 547 Broadway also appears on the bill for two sofas, two armchairs, four parlor chairs, one center table, and one étagère. A chair in the same pattern is in the Manney Collection (plate 12). It appears that very elaborately carved and pierced pieces were produced concurrently with unpierced pieces because the Belter company maintained the 547 Broadway address from 1852 until 1856. The evidence should end the speculation that solid-carved versus pierced-carved chairs were produced at different times as Belter's designs evolved.

It is clear, then, that Belter produced pierced-carved chairs for the Jordans in 1855. Belter's first patent, "Machinery for Sawing Arabesque Chairs," was issued July 31, 1847. Innovators seldom invent a device for which they have no use. Similarly, they are not likely to invent a device when they have not gained sufficient experience to refine an inspiration into a perfected model. Undoubtedly, Belter had made pierced chairbacks prior to 1847 or he would not have had the experience to develop the practical knowledge necessary for the 1847 patent; neither would he have been motivated to invent if the need had not arisen. A review of the patent language reveals a fact not integrally tied to the concept of the patent itself. The chairbacks were made separately from the rest of the chair or sofa and were not attached to the piece until after the back was cut into openwork. Directly tied to the description of the device is the fact that the chairbacks were curved, and that the cutting by the saw took place from the back of the chair toward the front. The use of such a device would result in openings whose boundaries are virtually perpendicular to the curved surface of the chairback.

A number of misconceptions have been promulgated regarding the nature of Belter's patents and also regarding methods for distinguishing Belter's work from that of his contemporaries. A common misunderstanding is that Belter patented the manufacture of laminated woods or plywood. None of the patents makes such a contention and, indeed, the February 23, 1858, patent, "Improvement in the Method of Manufacturing Furniture," contains a disclaimer, "I do not claim the simple pressing of veneers and glue between dies or cauls, one of which is convex and the other or others concave; nor do I claim the so gluing of veneers together that the grain of each stands at right angles to that of the next." Plywood is at least as old as the eighteenth century in England when it was used in furniture designs by Robert Adam. As is evident in the examples of chairs described earlier in this chapter, laminated-wood furniture originating from Belter's own hand had conclusively been put into the public domain at least as early as 1852, which predates the patent by six years.

The 1858 patent was for the production of laminated furniture that curves in two planes, rather than just one, to form the section of a sphere and for the method to accomplish its precise assembly. Stave construction is specifically mentioned for fashioning spherical-shape backs in this patent. Although it was possible and perhaps even likely that Belter experimented with lami-

3. Rear view of the spherical-shape back of a side chair showing the seams on the chairback, which are the borders of the adjacent staves. (*Collection of Dr. Milton Brindley*)

4. Side view of the chair in figure 3. The chair is curved in two planes with the upper chairback forming a portion of a sphere, as indicated by the applied line in the photograph. The chair is full size and follows the 1858 patent precisely. (*Collection of Dr. Milton Brindley*)

nated staves to produce some chairs that curved in one plane (to gain the experience and insights necessary to extend the technique to an extra geometrical dimension), the "ordinary manner" of producing them was to lay sheets with the grain at right angles and not to construct staves as an intermediary step. A chair made by Belter in the "ordinary way" is part of the Manney Collection (plate 18), and another done in the same pattern but according to the 1858 patent is in the private collection of Dr. Milton Brindley (figs. 3, 4).

The lack of understanding of the construction of Belter's furniture coupled with "Personal Experiences of an Old New York Cabinetmaker" have led many to the false conclusion that a seam on the back of a laminated chair implies that the piece is not by Belter but by a contemporary, Charles A. Baudouine. A man named Ernst Hagen came into the employ of the Charles Baudouine furniture business in 1853 and worked for that concern until around 1855. As an old man in 1908 Hagen produced his memoirs, in which he asserts that Baudouine made parlor suites with "round perforated backs . . . made of 5 layers of veneer glued up in a mould in one piece which made a very strong and not very heavy chair back only about 1/4 inch thick, all the ornamented carved work glued on after the perforated part of the thin back was sawed out and prepared." He further asserts that Baudouine avoided infringing on Belter's patent by "making the backs of 2 pieces with a center joint." Hagen drew a sketch of a chair showing a Baudouine chairback looking similar to those of Belter, but with a central seam through the entire piece. A cursory examination of a Belter chairback will probably result in the discovery of one or more subtle seams. If the chairs were made "in the ordinary manner," in Belter's language, the seams are simply the boundaries between adjacent sheets on the outer layer of veneer. Veneer cannot always be acquired in optimal widths, and several pieces may be required to cover a reasonably sized area. The seams are always vertical on the chairback, to facilitate the matching of the veneers and to give a more pleasing appearance. In some circumstances it appears definite that sheets of veneer cut from adjacent areas of a log were matched at the center of the chairback to form a distinguished and symmetrical figure about a center seam.

If the chair was made from stave construction as in Belter's 1858 patent, the seams penetrate two to three layers of veneer but no more. The appearance of a seam on a chairback, therefore, in no way disqualifies the chair as an example of Belter's work. As illustrated in the text of the 1858 patent, John Henry Belter had a fundamental understanding of the nature of pressed work and of the strength derived from it. If a chair were constructed of pressed work with a longitudinal

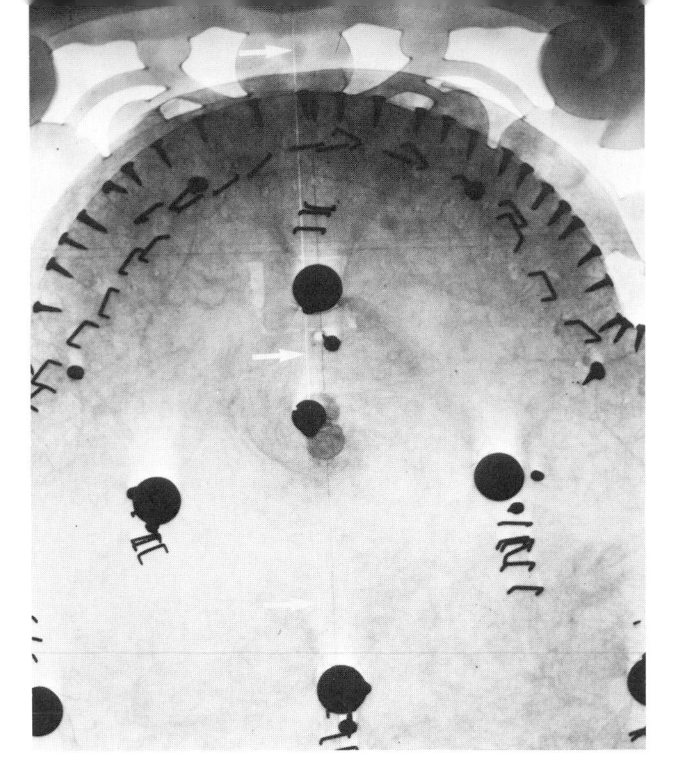

5. An X-ray photograph of a side chair with arrows marking the center seam passing through the entire chairback. The black circles along this line are metal fasteners; the other black dots are the buttons used for upholstery tufting. Also shown in black are upholstery staples and tacks. The upholstery material leaves a slight shadow above the tack impressions. (*Collection of Delores LePorte*)

seam through the entire chairback, the advantages of the laminating process would be significantly neutralized because inward pressure on either side of the back would cause stresses that could not be counteracted by the plywood construction. Although such a pressed-work process would have the advantage of facilitating the construction of curved sheets, the strains experienced at the center of the back would be the same as if two unlaminated boards were used. Clearly Belter would not have constructed such chairs, and the question remains whether or not someone else—perhaps Baudouine—would have.

Clare Vincent, writing for the 1973 *Winterthur Conference Annual,* points out that Belter's patent was published in 1858—three years after Hagen left Baudouine's shop and also three years after Baudouine's last business listing in Trow's *New York City Directory.* It is not likely that someone would have deliberately infringed on a patent that was as yet nonexistent. There would have been no infringement on the 1858 patent in any case as only stave construction of spherical-section chairbacks was claimed in the patent. Significant doubt is thus cast on the credibility of Hagen's memory. Perhaps Baudouine had pirated the device patented by Belter in 1847 for sawing openwork, and Hagen simply misunderstood the nature of the differences be-

6. Armchair, rosewood and ash. H. 48″, W. 27½″, D. 25″. This chair is in the same pattern as the ones in the parlor set in The Metropolitan Museum of Art, New York, which has been attributed to J. and J.W. Meeks. (*Photograph courtesy Western Reserve Historical Society, Cleveland, Ohio*)

tween Baudouine and Belter. In her 1973 work Vincent points out that "the only labeled examples of Baudouine's work that have come to light are a pair of card tables now in the collection of the Munson-Williams-Proctor Institute at Utica." The tables are of solid, not laminated, construction. Since 1973 a number of other examples have come to the authors' attention, including a parlor set, a worktable, a desk, and an étagère—none is laminated. Although no documentation accompanies it, a laminated rosewood chair in the collection of Delores LePorte meets Hagen's description of Baudouine's laminated parlor chairs. It is 37½ inches high and 19 inches wide. The seat depth is 16 inches, and the seat height from the floor is 12 inches. The chairback is curved, ⅜ inch thick, and made of five lamination of unequal thickness. An apparent seam runs down the center of the chairback. The use of X rays (fig. 5) has confirmed that the back is made of two pieces held together by metal fasteners under the upholstery. Light can be seen through a hairline separation of the seam near the top of the chair. The crest on the chair is applied to the top and back. No documentation on the provenance or origin of the chair is available.

It appears that links between laminated furniture and nineteenth-century cabinetmakers other than Belter are weak indeed. Some very significant structural differences exist among the laminated furniture that will be explored later in this chapter, but although it seems possible to identify furniture as non-Belter, it is not yet possible to attribute these pieces to a particular origin in many instances. One family of furniture that is significantly different from Belter's can be attributed through only a weak historical link. Apparently, Sophia Teresa Meeks, upon her marriage to Dexter A. Hawkins in 1859, was given a set of parlor furniture as a wedding gift. As Sophia was the daughter of Joseph W. Meeks, it has been accepted that the furniture was made at her father's furniture factory. The set is very similar to one in The Metropolitan Museum of Art in New York. Other chairs in the same pattern as the Meeks/Hawkins set can be found throughout the country (fig. 6).

In the 1856 patent for a laminated bed Belter provided direct evidence for precluding this type of laminated furniture utilizing thick veneers from being attributed to him. A detailed discussion of why this is so is contained in the section on tables later in this chapter.

Most labeled Meeks furniture comes from the era immediately preceding the Rococo Revival and resembles furniture found in the design book published by John Hall (*The Cabinet Makers' Assistant* [Baltimore, 1840; reprint ed., New York: National Superior, 1944]). The furniture establishes the transition from Empire to Victorian and was originally produced by Sophia's grandfather, Joseph Meeks. The differences between the furniture given to Sophia Meeks and that made by Belter are important to explore, for the family of laminated furniture to which it belongs comprises the largest assemblage of laminated furniture except for comparable quantities in the Belter group. Before this study can evolve to that point, a digression that ex-

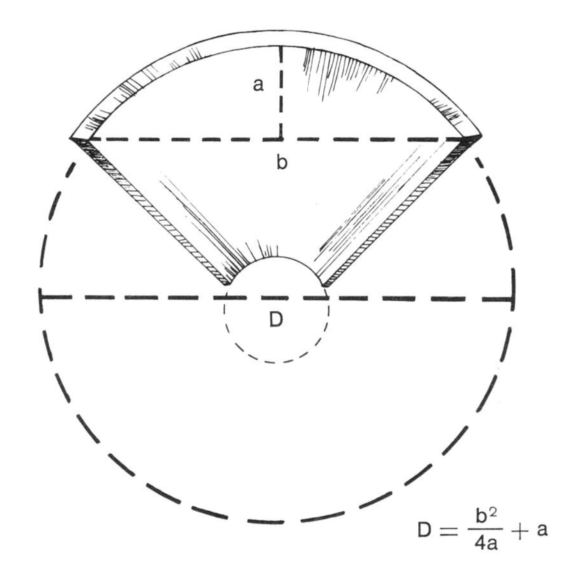

7. Schematic drawing of a chairback to show how the size of the cauls was measured.

plores Belter's work through the 1858 patent is appropriate.

First of all Belter says, "Pressed work is invariably composed entirely of veneers and glue. The grain of each veneer is laid at right angles to that of the next." Some pressed-work examples, however, do not have the grain of each veneer laid at right angles to the next. Examples can be found where the grain of succeeding layers make an angle of somewhat less than 90 degrees with each other. Still other examples can be found where some layers have the grain running parallel to at least one other adjacent layer. Such a piece could have been created by an apprentice not fully skilled or trained in the proper Belter techniques; or, on the other hand, such furniture was not made at the Belter factory. As this characteristic appears to be rather consistent within a family of non-Belter furniture, it appears that some other cabinetmaker found virtue in pressed work with the grain parallel in some of the adjacent veneer layers.

In another context Belter says, "Pressed work has consequently been curved only in one plane, so that each part forms a portion of a hollow cylinder or cone." A clue is given here to the geometrical nature of Belter's chairbacks. By the careful measurement of the back, it should be possible to describe the caul in which the chairback was pressed. Using a flexible tool that conforms to the shape of the chairback, both the chord across the curve and its depth can be measured (fig. 7). If *b* is the chord and *a* the depth of the back, then the diameter of the caul that produced the chairback can be determined at a given point on the chairback by simple geometry. Calculating the diameter at various points along the chairback then reveals the vertical shape of the caul. If the diameter does not vary between the bottom of the chairback and the top, the caul was in the shape of a cylinder. If the diameter grows or diminishes linearly along the height of the back, the caul was in the shape of a cone. The cone can further be defined to determine how steep it was by using some three-dimensional geometry.

If D_s is the radius of the caul at its widest part and D_h is the radius at a narrower part, and H is the distance measured along the back (fig. 8) of the chair between the points where D_s and D_h are measured, then the angle α, which defines the steepness of the cone, is given by

$$\alpha = \cos^{-1}\left[\frac{1D_s - D_h1}{2H}\right]$$

The careful measurement of chairs using the above derivations can help determine if the same machinery was used to produce a given pressed chairback. It is not thoroughly clear if several chairbacks were fashioned at one time and then cut apart or if the cauls were limited in size to produce one chairback at a time. The 1858 patent suggests that eight backs could be made at once and then cut apart after the layers of veneer had been glued together. Some could have been right side up and others upside down to fit them together in such a way as to conserve wood. A similar scenario could be applied to chairbacks produced in a cylindrical caul, but in a conical caul either the top or bottom of the back would have had a more acute curvature and no consistency would have been possible without requiring the same orientation of all the pieces produced.

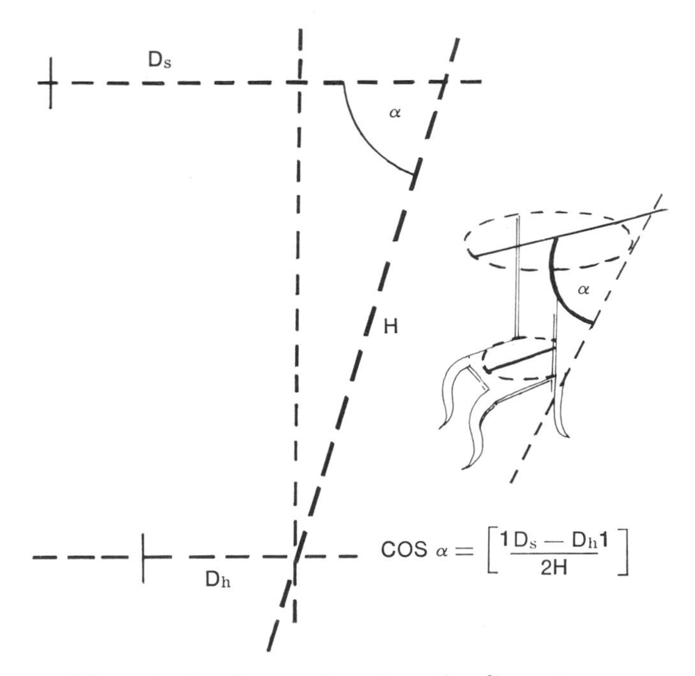

8. Schematic drawing to show how the dimensions of the cauls were calculated.

Nonetheless, being an innovative craftsman, it could be expected that Belter would have attempted to build chairbacks in this manner with the use of a conical caul. Such an example exists in the Manney Collection (plate 19). The angle α for this chair is 95 degrees (that is, more acutely bent at the top than at the bottom), whereas a virtually identical chair in the possession of one of the authors, Dr. Stanek, has an angle α of 85 degrees. From these data it is evident that some chairbacks were made from conical cauls while oriented in opposite directions to minimize the amount of rosewood wasted (fig. 9).

Numerous examples of seating furniture exist with solid crests that are carved and applied to the laminated chairback (plate 19, fig. 10). Although no applied-crest examples of this type have been documented with a bill of sale or a label, detailed examination of such examples has yielded significant results regarding their attribution. They are constructed with laminated backs with the orientation of the veneers alternating perpen-

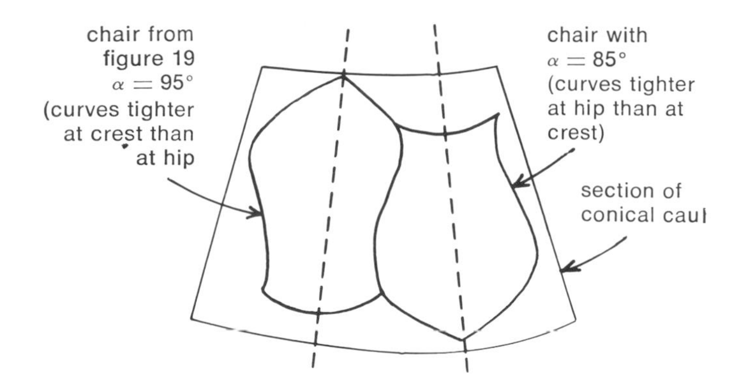

9. An illustration of how chairbacks were cut out to minimize waste.

dicularly through seven to nine layers. These veneers range in thickness from 0.04 inch (1 mm) to 0.07 inch (1.8 mm) with an average of 0.055 inch (1.4 mm). This compares to documented Belter pieces with an average veneer thickness of 0.062 inch (1.6 mm), ranging from 0.05 (1.3 mm) to 0.07 inch (1.8 mm). The angle α for applied-crest pieces varies slightly and is clustered around 80 degrees, which is remarkably similar to the documented pieces of similar design. A family of well-executed applied-crest seating furniture represented in the Manney Collection (plate 21, figs. 11, 12) displays the same construction techniques, style, and selection of naturalistic motifs as do documented pieces.

The authors believe that these applied-crest pieces were constructed by Belter for varied reasons. The laminated chairbacks were constructed with from seven to nine veneers of 0.055-inch average thickness and had angle α's generally measuring between 78 degrees and 82 degrees, paralleling documented seating furniture. The laminated chairback forms the back seat-rail with tapered rear legs that are nearly rectangular in cross section inset slightly from the back seat-rail. The front legs and the vertical arm brace on armchairs are generally of one piece of wood, as previously reported by Clare Vincent. Armchairs also demonstrate a mechanically efficient joint, most likely a secret (double-lap) dovetail, between the horizontal and vertical portions of the

10. An X-ray photograph of an applied crest showing how the crest is applied without dowels. Repair work is visible on the right side of the crest.

11. Front view of the chair in plate 21.

12. Rear view of the chair in plate 21.

arms, paralleling documented pieces. Even the casters, when original, are found to be of the brass platform type with hollow brass rollers.

The designs of this family of applied-crest chairs parallel designs by Belter done without applied crests. Likewise the selection of naturalistic motifs and the execution of these motifs form a conclusive parallel, especially the handling of carved roses, acorns, and leaves. Notably, the various naturalistic motifs are more open than in documented pieces, which is principally because the use of elongated vines and stems creates greater amounts of open space carved into the chairbacks.

In addition to showing this family of applied-crest pieces to be Belter in origin, it can be reasonably concluded that Belter executed these pieces during the 1840s and early 1850s prior to large-scale production, which began in 1854. This conclusion is supported by a number of facts. When reupholstering Belter furniture, newspapers are frequently found attached to the inner side of the chairback. These newspapers originally had the purpose of protecting the outer veneers from the marring caused by metal cauls and also making easier the job of dislodging the chairbacks from the caul upon the drying of the glue, a technique familiar to all experienced woodworkers. Now they serve as chronological benchmarks for investigators. Two chairs with applied crests in the Manney Collection were found to have such newspapers with established dates of 1849.

13. Armchair with newspaper fragments in the chairback. (*Manney Collection*)

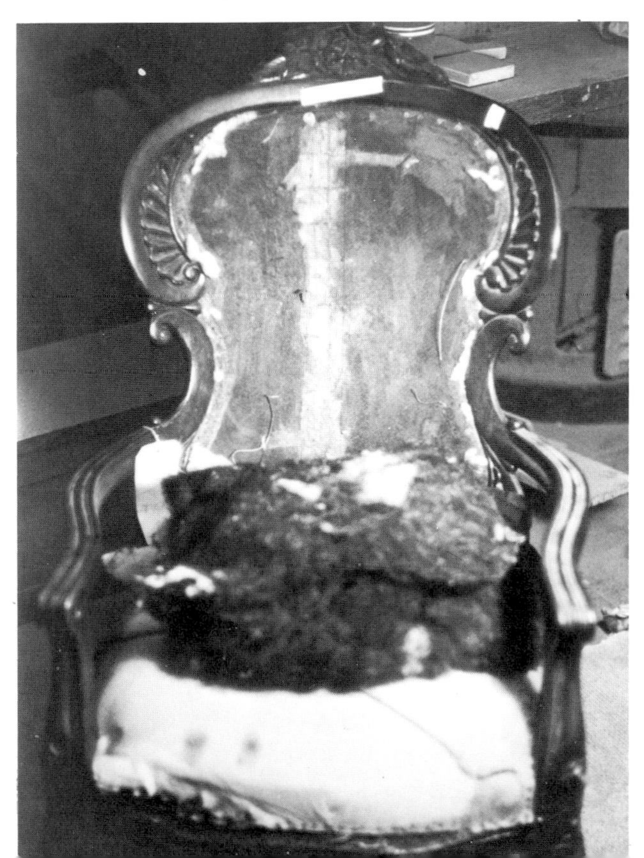

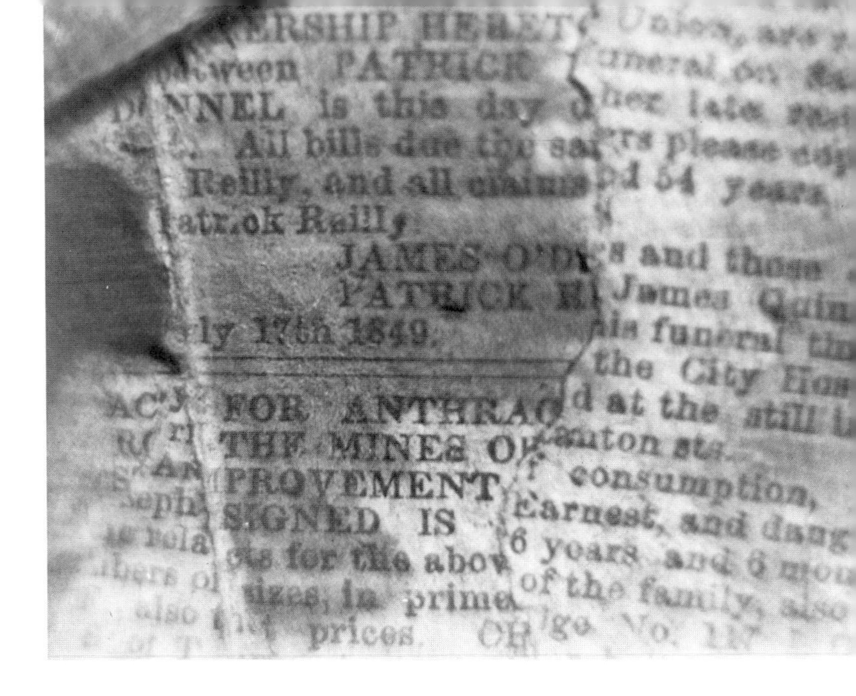

ERSHIP HERET
tween PATRICK
NNEL is this day d
All bills due the sa
Reilly, and all claims
atrick Reilly
JAMES O'D
PATRICK R
ly 17th 1849.
FOR ANTHRAC
THE MINES OF
PROVEMENT
SIGNED IS
ts for the abov
sizes, in prime
prices.

funeral on
her late
rs please
d 54 years
s and those
James Quin
his funeral
the City Ho
d at the still
anton st
consumption,
Earnest, and dang
6 years and 6 mon
of the family, also

14. Detail showing newsprint.

15. Side chair showing exposed back with newsprint.

Dating from incomplete newspaper fragments can be very misleading. The authors have found a 1789 date relating to George Washington and birth dates in obituaries, which are obviously also misleading. However, if used with care, the method can prove to be of value. One of the Manney chairs (fig. 13) is lined with a newspaper displaying a public notice of bankruptcy (fig. 14) dated July 17, 1849; obviously such notices are current with the publication in which they appear. On another Manney chair (fig. 15) two public notices of 1849 appear. One is the announcement of a

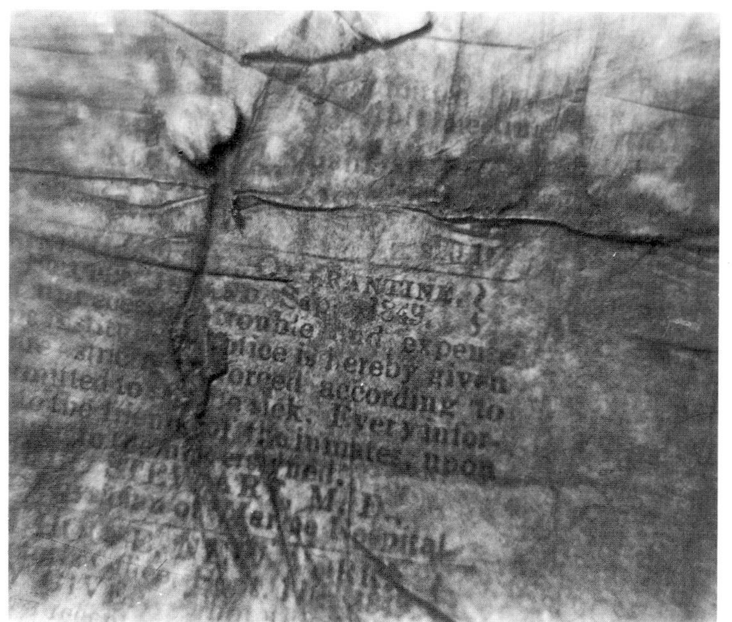

16. Detail showing newsprint.

17. Detail showing newsprint.

quarantine (fig. 16); the other announces the publication of short stories by William Thackeray (fig. 17).

Other means of dating these pieces were the consistently high quality of the carving and the rarity of extant examples of this family of applied-crest pieces. It could be expected that, as a cabinetmaker producing "made-to-order" furniture in small quantities, Belter would have made pieces consistent in character and quality. As the manager of a factory Belter had to employ many other individuals, whose attempts at reproducing a Belter design displayed personal interpretations varying in quality and character among the carvers. The evidence leads to the conclusion that applied-crest Belter furniture is typical of his earlier work, principally done by his own hand or under his close supervision.

There are examples of applied-crest seating furniture that do not fit the descriptions cited above and are therefore of questionable attribution. The carving on such examples is generally in much lower relief and less naturalistic; however, the means of construction does not differ substantially from the family of applied-crest furniture cited above. One unusual feature found on some applied-crest furniture of both types is a laminated chairback that extends to form the entire laminated side rail. Note an example of this type of construction found in the Manney Collection in plate 9.

A mahogany sofa in the Manney Collection (plate 35) is also believed to have an origin earlier in Belter's career. The use of mahogany in itself is evidence of construction in the 1840s, because of the popularity of that wood prior to the Rococo Revival. Many examples of Belter's work have solid applied wood added to laminated construction for the purpose of additional carved relief; however, the sofa is laminated throughout most of the high-relief carving. This is indeed rare, and the only other examples observed with this type of construction are found in a suite of furniture in this pattern at Fountain Elms, part of the Munson-Williams-Proctor Institute in Utica, New York. These examples have sixteen laminations at their thickest part compared to eight laminations plus applied wood at the corresponding place in the Jordan pieces done in the same pattern.

An anomaly found in this and one other sofa in the Manney Collection (plate 33) is the flared or beveled piercing of the chairback. The flaring opens toward the reverse side of the chairback. This could have been done as an aesthetic measure to make the backs appear more open-carved when viewed from the side, or the flaring may have resulted from the misguided use of Belter's sawing apparatus (patented in 1847) or from the lack of its use. The orientation of a chairback in the sawing apparatus, as illustrated in the patent, would have resulted in splintering on the reverse side of the chairback from the sawing motion with the blade in backward unless suitable precautions were taken. If the latter assumption is correct, then seating furniture exhibiting such flaring was probably among the first to be pierced-carved.

The Vietor parlor set in the Museum of the City of New York as well as one of the parlor sets in the Texas governor's mansion exhibit this type of flaring.

TABLE 1

DOCUMENTED BELTER PARLOR FURNITURE

ROSALIE PATTERN [1]

	Armchair	Side chair (A)	Side chair (B)
height	43″	37.25″	37.25″
width	23″	18″	18″
depth	21″	18″	18″
seat height	13″	13.50″	13.50″
D_s [2]	35.50″	24.50″	25.50″
D_h [3]	27.80″	19.50″	20.90″
α [4]	74°	79°40′	80°30′
number of laminations	7	7	7
thickness of chairback	0.494″	0.415″	0.415″

JORDAN BROTHERS SETS

	Parlor Set A				Parlor Set B		
	Large settee	Small settee	Arm-chair	Side chair	Small settee	Arm-chair	Side chair
height	....	....	43″	38″	45″	44″	38″
width	....	....	23″	19″	55″	23.50″	19″
depth	....	....	22″	17.50″	....	21.50″	17″
seat height	....	....	12″	12.50″	11″	12.50″	13″
D_s [2]	....	....	27.80″	21.40″	....	27.10″	23.50″
D_h [3]	....	....	27.80″	20″	....	26.20″	19.30″
α [4]	....	....	90°	86°50′	....	88°	80°
number of laminations	8	8	8	7	8	8	8
thickness of chairback	0.528″	0.547″	0.438″	0.369″	0.45″	0.45″	0.45″

[1] *Not the set at Rosalie.*

[2] *Diameter of the caul (mold) as measured at the shoulder.*

[3] *Diameter of the caul (mold) as measured at the hip.*

[4] *The angle describing the vertical sloping of the caul, with 90° being a perfect cylinder.*

Besides the parallel mentioned earlier of seating furniture design with solid applied crests and those with laminated nonapplied crests, there is a second parallel worthy of discussion and illustration. There are several basic designs of Belter furniture devoid of naturalistic carved embellishments. An example is in the Manney Collection (plate 18). Note the resemblance between plates 18, 2, and 5. Plate 5 is an elaborate pierced-carved example in the Manney Collection that has the same outline of form as the unpierced Rosalie pattern, plate 2, which in turn is a further embellishment of that shown in plate 18. Plate 18 is the basic chair with the pear-shaped outline and no further carving.

This logical progression of a simple design into more elaborate patterns is not unusual in Belter's work. There is even an additional stage between plates 18 and 2 that is not illustrated.

The second most common example of this parallel

is the design found in plate 20, which forms a stylized figure eight in the chairback. The detailed examination of seating furniture that has a common shape and design yields no different construction techniques or abnormal variations in veneer thickness or angle αs. In other words there is no more variation in construction between successive patterns with a common overall shape and design than there is between individual pieces within the same pattern. Each piece with a similar overall design, even with a differing degree of embellishment, was made in either the same caul or a duplicate caul.

With regard to materials it is obvious with some study that Belter made chairs using exterior woods of rosewood, oak, and mahogany. He does express a preference in the 1858 patent, however. "In short, the veneers, . . . which, when the work is in place, are exhibited to the observer on the front side, and the veneers . . . which are shown on the back side, should be rose-wood [*sic*], or the like highly-prized wood, while all the rest may be oak, hickory, blackwalnut, or other cheap wood." The secondary wood most commonly found is ash, with maple and mahogany frequently seen on cabinet pieces.

TABLES

A variety of Belter tables exists with documentation to support their authenticity. A solid table devoid of laminations with quite elaborate carving is part of the Manney Collection (plate 55). On the inside of the table apron can be found the Belter label (plate 55a) indicating the Third Avenue and 76th Street address as well as the 552 Broadway address. A round table in the Museum of the City of New York bears the same label on the upper part of a leg. This table is round with elaborate pierced-carved detail. Its multicolored marble is somewhat of an anomaly because most Belter tables are capped with pure white marble, although a few wooden-top examples may also be found. Each of the Jordan parlor sets contains a white marble turtle-top table—again with elaborate pierced carving. These tables have faces sculpted and applied to the center of the long aprons on two sides of the tables. The identity of the images is unknown.

Another pierced-carved table with a white marble top in The Newark Museum has tacked beneath the apron a label with the 547 Broadway Belter address and the words "Cabinet Manufacturer." A similar table in the Manney Collection (plate 48) bears no label.

In the examples discussed above and others observed by the authors, a variety of design and construction can be found. Laminations, laminations plus blocks, and solid work all appear. Round, scalloped, and cabochon-shape tops are seen. Pierced work and solid work are just as common. Tables with openwork bear only a few C- or S-scrolls, while the bulk of the apron carvings depict flowers, grape clusters, and realistic leaves, vines, and branches. The naturalistic branches used to connect the various carved floral and fruit elements sharply contrast with the baroque C-scrolls found connecting similar elements in the family of tables produced to complement the seating furniture suspected of being produced by the Meeks factory.

Belter tables that are laminated have each lamination approximately 0.06 inch (1.5 mm) thick. Belter tables seem to be unique in character, relative to the seating furniture that they accompany, with no apparent attempt to match table design with a given pattern of seating furniture. About the only consistency that appears seems to be that pierced-carved tables generally went with pierced-carved parlor chairs, whereas solid-carved tables were paired with solid-carved chairs.

Well-documented pieces in museums, the Manney Collection, and other private collections form the nucleus for the attribution of undocumented tables.

Three major families of laminated tables have been found to exist: a thickly laminated version weakly attributed to the Meeks factory, and two families of thinly laminated tables. One family of the latter group is by Belter, whereas the other is possibly by Belter but of unknown documented origin at this time.

The thickly laminated group has aprons and stretchers consisting of five laminations with an average veneer thickness of 0.13 inch (3.3 mm). The stretcher comprises two molded pieces in the shape of a C oriented in support of the table legs, with the convex sides adjacent. This configuration creates a very strong support for the table while the center finial conceals the two-piece construction of the stretcher. No documented or even supposed Belter table possesses a laminated stretcher. The stretchers of the tables attributed to Belter share common features of design and are always carved from solid wood. The center finials on the stretchers of thickly laminated tables always have carved fruit and nuts, never flowers. This is not true of documented Belter tables, which have center finials adorned by flowers, fruits, and nuts.

The carvings on the aprons of these thickly laminated tables parallel specific patterns of thickly laminated seating furniture not only in the use of specific motifs but also in overall complexity of design. Two such tables are found in the Manney Collection. One table has a cabochon-shape top (plate 49), with a design paralleling the seating furniture said to have been given as a wedding gift to Sophia Meeks Hawkins. The other table has an oval top, and its design parallels the concept employed in a set of furniture as described by Ed Polk Douglas, former curator at The Strong Museum, Rochester, New York, in an article published in *The New York-Pennsylvania Collector* in 1979.

Although most pierced-carved Belter table aprons are entirely of laminated construction, exceptions exist. Applied solid wood is occasionally added to the base of the table apron to provide more depth to that component. Examples can be found in the Manney Collection (plate 48) as well as the documented, round Belter table in the Museum of the City of New York.

Although individuality is a trademark of tables described as Belter, after detailed measurement and examination the authors can judge with reasonable certainty that the tables in plates 46, 48, 53, and 54 are a product of Belter's factory. All of these tables have ten laminations comprising the apron and average 0.055 inch (1.4 mm) per lamination. The three most credible documented and laminated tables in the Museum of the City of New York, The Newark Museum, and the Texas governor's mansion have been measured and average 0.065, 0.065, and 0.063 inch (1.65 mm, 1.65 mm, 1.60 mm) per lamination, respectively. The table in plate 52 bears the Belter label and the table in plate 47 meets all the stylistic and construction prerequisites for being called Belter, including ties to similar tables purchased for Tuthill King's town house in Chicago and for Rosalie in Natchez, Mississippi. The tables in plates 49 and 50, although laminated, are not attributed to Belter.

The third classification of laminated tables is the rarest and most enigmatic. Paralleling in style the laminated seating furniture in collections of the Smithsonian Institution and The Bayou Bend in Houston, this style is exemplified by thin laminations; less naturalistic carving; delicate and interwoven pierced-carved vines, and an ogee-curved, laminated stretcher. Veneers on this classification of tables are 0.059 to 0.066 inch (1.5 mm to 1.7 mm) in thickness, with usually seven laminations incorporating the apron and nine laminations incorporating the stretcher. Although this last class of table is the rarest, it should be noted that Belter-classified tables are much less prevalent than those of the thickly laminated variety.

The motif carved on the short ends of the Jordan tables is identical within "craftsman's error" to a table accompanying a laminated parlor set made for the Chicago town house of Tuthill King in the nineteenth century. Now the property of the Chicago Historical Society, the set completely satisfies all of the applicable requirements for the full attribution of Belter seating furniture. Paralleling the use of the sculpted heads on the Jordan tables, the Tuthill King table displays the likeness of George Washington on one side and Benjamin Franklin on the other. Some important features of the Tuthill King tables are the heads of animals carved on the legs above the table feet. One each of eagle, dolphin, panther, and dog are meticulously executed in rosewood. The same faces appear on the legs of two matching tables at Rosalie. The aprons of these tables are made of rectangular blocks with two thin outer laminations. There is no openwork on these tables, but splendid carvings cover the bottom part of the table in a very tasteful fashion. A similar table (plate 47) is in the Manney Collection, where the animal sculptures appear to be a dolphin, an eagle, and two horses.

As evidence that Belter distributed his furniture outside the New York–area retail market, the White House possesses a bill of sale for a table bought by President Lincoln in 1861 from Wm. H. Carryl & Bros. in Philadelphia. The table, now in the Lincoln Bedroom, is of laminated rosewood with an apron virtually identical to the labeled Belter table in the Museum of the City of New York.

It is obvious that the manufacture of laminated tables of any design, because of the incorporation of pressed work, necessitated the use of specialized equipment, namely cauls, to manufacture the table aprons. Although the fabrication of a pressed-work table requires great skill, the design and building of a caul involves even greater skill, because the concept of the finished table product must first be considerably refined as a precondition of constructing the caul and because the cauls themselves require refinement before a satisfactory laminated table can be produced. Having a specific knowledge of the caul design is not very important for tables of the thickly laminated variety because of the close tie previously discussed between tables and matched seating furniture and because many such tables are virtually duplicates of each other. However, in the case of Belter tables, it appears that, with few exceptions, each one bears no specific similarity to a given pattern of seating furniture. Meticulously measuring documented Belter tables for the purpose of re-creating the cauls employed in their fabrication in their original sizes provides specific evidence of Belter attribution. Caul analysis for the variety of tables produced, however, requires a detailed accounting of the connection between the legs and the laminated apron pieces, a discounting of applied wood glued to the base of some laminated aprons, and requires the removal of the marble tops for appropriate observation because considerable variation is found in the dimensions of the cut marble. To illustrate this last point, the two Belter consoles (plates 53, 54) in the Manney Collection have identical dimensions for length, depth, and height (without casters), yet the marble tops are far from being duplicates. A thorough caul analysis for the tables would result in a basis for attribution similar to that developed for seating furniture. If a table possesses the basic attributes of Belter design and is fashioned from either laminations or blocks and laminations, a simpler approach to establishing authenticity is the analysis of the thickness of the laminated veneers.

A detailed examination of documented tables plus

undocumented counterparts attributed to Belter by the authors reveals that the mean lamination thickness is 0.057 inch (1.45 mm) with a maximum deviation from the mean of ±15 percent. The variation is caused in part by the method of manufacturing the veneer and in part from the variation in glue thickness between layers of wood. The mean thickness for an individual piece of veneer is found by measuring the overall thickness of a laminated section with vernier calipers, subtracting the thickness of the applied carving, and dividing that thickness by the number of laminations. The mean thickness of all laminations is then found by averaging the mean thickness of laminations from individual pieces of furniture. The amount of glue between two sections of veneer affects the measurements slightly: it fills in voids between veneers that cannot be perfectly pressed together. Measurements can be refined by using a microscope but it is not necessary as the deviations are within ±15 percent of the mean using the method described above. Lamination thicknesses for tables correspond to lamination thicknesses in documented seating furniture, as described earlier in this chapter. The thickly laminated tables belonging to the family of furniture ascribed by many experts to the Meeks brothers have mean lamination thicknesses of 0.126 inch (3.2 mm), ±15 percent. In his 1856 "Bedstead" patent Belter suggests that "The veneers . . . may as well be a little thicker than ordinary, say, about 0.0625 inch thick." This statement is testimony to the fact that 0.0625 inch (1.6 mm) is the thickest veneer that he would employ and thus conclusively eliminates the possibility that the prolific family of furniture with a mean lamination thickness of 0.126 inch (3.2 mm) could be Belter's—especially if such furniture was made prior to 1856. The aprons on the two types of tables vary by 33 percent in overall thickness, but the different number of laminations brings the veneer thickness variance between the two types of furniture to 120 percent. Belter tables have aprons constructed with seven to ten laminations, whereas the so-called Meeks tables have aprons made of five to six laminations, in the experience of the authors.

Without a label or bill of sale no piece of furniture can be attributed to any cabinetmaker without some suspicion. The above combination of technical analysis and strong circumstantial evidence should be adequate for a jury of experts to authenticate many tables presumed to have been made by Belter. As the body of knowledge surrounding laminated furniture grows, the remaining tables may someday be able to be attributed with the same authority.

BEDS

The bedstead fabricated according to the patent of August 19, 1856, is unique among the beds produced during the nineteenth century. The beds of no other cabinetmaker can be confused with the beds of Belter. Although their aesthetic beauty is worthy of marvel, practical considerations motivated their evolution.

> One object of my invention is to surmount this difficulty [the use of peculiar wrenches and considerable time to disassemble], and allow the parts to be immediately separated without tools [in case of fire] . . . Again the ordinary bedstead contains deep and intricate recesses about the joints and fastenings which are difficult of access and notorious as hiding places for bugs. A second object of my invention is to avoid the necessity for these recesses. Again the thickness of the posts and other parts in ordinary bedsteads intrudes upon what would otherwise be valuable space either on their interior or exterior faces. A third object of my invention is to avoid this evil. And again an ordinary veneered bedstead is liable to contain empty spaces between the veneer and the solid wood in which spaces young bugs may be concealed. These spaces result from inequalities in the "calls" [*sic*] as the large molds are turned which press the veneer upon the solid wood. . . . A fourth object of my invention is to avoid this evil.

Belter beds consist of curved and pressed laminated woods, have self-supporting headboards and footboards held together by dowels or brass hooks, with glue to fill all voids to resolve the "evils." He preferred to make the bed in two pieces: a headboard and a footboard, each of which curves toward the other, forming half of each side rail. Belter acknowledges that the bedstead can also be made in four pieces; four-piece beds have side rails that connect to the footboard and the headboard.

Only one two-piece bed has been observed. Most surviving beds are made in four pieces, contrary to the preference Belter stated in the patent for two-piece construction. Beds were apparently made in different sizes and intricacy of decoration. A twin-size bed can be found in the Gene Weber–Durell Armstrong collection. A two-piece bed stamped "J. H. Belter patented August 19, 1856, NY," exists in another American private collection. The headboard on this piece is low and no carving whatsoever is employed. A bed with a high headboard supporting two putti (similar to those in plate 57 of the Manney Collection) is part of the Charles and Linda Primrose collection. A fabulous pierced-carved bed with open carving of vines, acorns, and cherub heads is in the collection in The Brooklyn Museum. There are three Belter beds in the Manney Collection (plates 57, 58, 59). One of these beds is magnificent. Lavish carvings of flowers and nuts mark the connections between the side rails and the headboard and footboard. A lion holding a leafy branch is centered on each side rail. Two putti accompany birds, C-scrolls, and flowers in the open carving that crests the headboard.

Another unique factor incorporated into the construction of these beds is the serpentine shape of the headboards and footboards as well as the side rails. This design innovation was facilitated by the lamination process and has resulted in the unusual shape of the box springs employed for support of the mattress. The patent provides for a further use of the planks supporting the springs as a brace to hold together the independent headboard and footboard structures. This is done through incorporation of a tapered projection on the bed with a complementary cutout in the support for the box springs. As mentioned in the patent and as observed by the authors, the support of the mattress and the stable interconnection of the side rails can also be accomplished with projecting ledges at the corners of the bed and wedged cross-member planks.

The number of laminations on the beds varies from sixteen to twenty-four on the scrolling that envelops the bed. Some beds have four feet (one at each corner, and others have six (when an additional foot is at the center of the rail on each side). In all cases the feet are broad based and conform to the curvature of the bed. Also, it is common to have rosewood scrollwork outlining the feet as in the case of all the beds in the Manney Collection. The bed in The Brooklyn Museum has more architecturally designed feet and is in that sense unique. The Brooklyn Museum bed is also unique in that it was pierced-carved to be observed from all angles, that is, it has been beautifully carved on both sides of the footboard and the headboard.

Although decorative carving varies considerably among laminated beds, the overall means of construction, thickness of veneers (0.06 inch or 1.5 mm), and types of woods do not vary. The same difficulty in attribution encountered with seating furniture is not usual with laminated beds. All those that have been observed have been uniquely Belter in making full use of the lamination process to further aesthetic as well as practical purposes. Although only a single bed that dutifully follows the patent description has been observed, all others, including the three beds in the Manney Collection, parallel closely the directions Belter provides in his 1856 patent.

BUREAUS

Although sideboards and other special cabinet furniture may be the rarest type of furniture produced by Belter, the rarest among the patented pieces is the bureau. Belter's patents for chairs and beds were issued in 1847, 1856, and 1858. The bureau patent was issued in 1860, just three years before Belter's death. Again, the Belter bureau is an example of beautiful furniture at its finest, but practicality was the motivation for its development.

The locking mechanism was devised to make it possible to lock or unlock all the drawers when locking just the top drawer. Springs made it possible to keep one drawer of the bureau open while the others remained locked and to lock the open drawer by simply pushing it into its normal closed position.

All of the drawers were constructed using one piece of pressed work and cutting the other drawers from the resulting cylinder. Thus, by eliminating the need for stretchers through the use of drawer bottom extensions fitted into grooves in the sides of the case, the bureau could be made to have continuity in the front as if it were made from one piece of wood.

One very important aspect of laminated work is mentioned in the patent. That is, pressed work, as Belter produced it, bent toward the concave side by itself upon removal from a caul, altering its own curvature. This factor is important in the consideration of chair caul diameters discussed under "Seating Furniture" earlier in this chapter. The diameters measured there are appropriate for matching chairbacks manufactured in the same device. All would have been subjected to the same process, were made of the same material, and were of the same size. They would thus be expected to change their shape uniformly. It should be noted, however, that the "virtual" caul diameters used for that analysis are different from the real caul diameters measured on the caul itself. This change is not very significant in chair construction because the chairbacks form small arcs that are then attached to seat-rails. For the bureau the drawer sides close on each other. The sum of the interior angles of the drawer must be 360 degrees and the sides must make right angles with the back. Belter therefore had to design a caul so that the large angles would shrink to 90 degrees when the drawer was removed from the caul. If the geometry in the patent drawings is correct, the drawer back made of six laminations would close from 102 degrees with the side in the caul to 90 degrees when removed. The drawer front made of ten laminations would have closed from 98 degrees with the side in the caul to 90 degrees when removed.

Not only the drawers of patented bureaus were laminated, so were the dividers inserted in the top drawer (plate 60), the sides of the bureau cabinet, the drawer molding, and the various decorations surrounding the mirror. The bureau in the Manney Collection follows precisely the description in the patent. Although the crest is 95 inches (2.4 m) from the floor, it is carved with flowers, grapes, leaves, and acorns with the same intricacy as if it appeared at eye level.

An in-depth study of Belter patent bureaus to distinguish them from those of competitors is not necessary. Belter's pieces are uniquely distinctive in mechanical operation, and the patent afforded protection from others' copying their workings for financial gain.

THE BASIC FACTS AND SOME THEORIES ABOUT JOHN HENRY BELTER'S ORIGINS

Marvin D. Schwartz

Very little is known about John Henry Belter outside of his career as a furniture maker. No references to general activities as a member of a church, of a social organization, or as a citizen have been found. We might then assume that his business was his primary concern. The Dun reports, already mentioned, evaluated J.H. Belter & Co. as a good credit risk, even in years when the furniture business was bad. The reporter at Dun was critical of the high quality of Belter's production because he believed that it kept profits down. In the 1850s competitors like J. and J.W. Meeks were able to invest in real estate with the higher profits they made by producing less fine furniture.

Information about John Henry Belter's origins have been garnered from interviews with members of the family rather than from the study of documents like a birth certificate and immigration papers. Only a death notice and a will provide documentary evidence to confirm family tradition. Born in 1804 in Ulm, Württemberg (now Baden-Württemberg), he is said to have arrived in the United States in 1840. The first evidence of his residence in New York is the listing "John H. Belter cabinetmaker 40½ Chatham St." in the New York City Directories for 1844.

Belter arrived in the United States as an adult, and more than likely he was already fully trained and experienced as a cabinetmaker. There is every reason to believe he learned his trade in his native city, Ulm, which is on the Danube at the foot of the Swabian Jura, roughly equidistant from Stuttgart, the capital of the Kingdom of Württemberg when Belter was born, and Munich, the capital of Bavaria. Both were cities of cultural significance in the early nineteenth century when Belter was a youth. As an apprentice learning cabinetmaking he must have made classical furniture in the Empire style. In the 1830s he might very well have seen the beginnings of the Rococo Revival in German-speaking areas. The style had begun to attract interest in France and England by the 1820s. The beginning of the reign of Charles X in 1824 is regarded as the start of the Rococo Revival, although it is possible to find isolated examples earlier. In the light of Belter's approach to the rococo, which we shall see includes the use of seventeenth-century motifs for decoration, it is interesting to find that the first references to the style call it *Louis XIV*. In the 1828 edition of George Smith's *Cabinet Maker's and Upholsterer's Guide, Louis XIV* is used to characterize a plate illustrating a Rococo Revival style interior, and the plate illustrating a chair titled "French Antique Chair" is described in the text as "after the taste of the Age of Louis XIV" (figs. 18, 19). Although German furniture makers could have used English and French books, related designs do not appear in the German publications until the 1830s when such periodicals as Wilhelm Kimbel's *Journal für Möbelschreiner und Tapeziner* (1837) included rococo designs in books that were predominantly Empire with some suggestions in the Gothic Revival style (figs. 20, 21). Although 1837 saw Kimbel using Louis XIV and Louis XV "French" designs, there were also an overwhelming number of Empire or Biedermeier designs used that year. In the same volume as the rococo designs, plate 3 (fig. 22) is typically Empire style with minor but glaring exceptions in the valance of the bed. The hanging is cut in a pattern that must have been inspired by the late seventeenth-century designs of the Anglo-Dutch architect Daniel Marot, and the valance topping the hanging is in a Rococo Revival pattern inspired by eighteenth-century models. For Belter, then, Rococo Revival designs were available as logical sources of inspiration at about the time he was preparing to migrate.

There is another matter to consider: the changes in designs between the eighteenth and the nineteenth century. Comparing the Kimbel chair design to an eighteenth-century chair made in Paris (fig. 23), the transition from rococo to Rococo Revival is striking. Kimbel defined details with a clarity characteristic of the nineteenth century, whereas the eighteenth-century rococo chair has the details carved beautifully but more simply. The eighteenth-century French craftsman captured the spirit of leaves, the essence of the motif, but

18. Illustration of a Louis XIV interior from George Smith, *The Cabinet Maker's and Upholsterer's Guide* (London: Jones & Co., 1828), plate CLII.

19. Illustration of a "French Antique Chair," Smith, *The Cabinet Maker's and Upholsterer's Guide,* plate CXLVI.

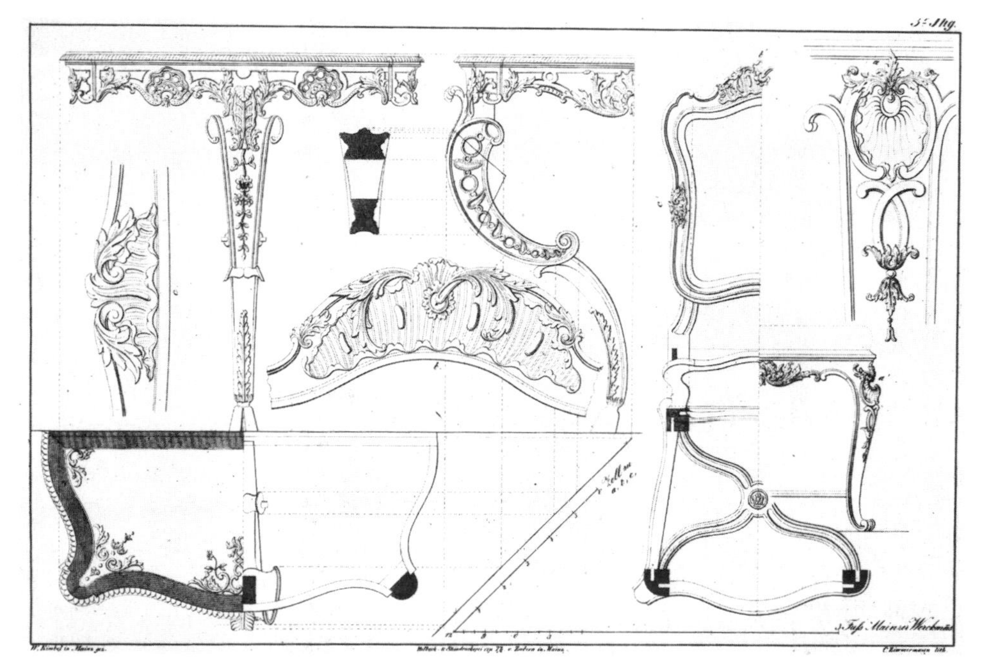

20. Drawings of a chair from Wilhelm Kimbel, *Journal für Möbelschreiner und Tapeziner,* vol. 19 (1837), detail of plate 9. (*The Metropolitan Museum of Art, New York; The Elisha Whittelsey Fund, 1968*)

21. Illustration of an interior from Kimbel, *Journal für Möbelschreiner,* plate 9. (*The Metropolitan Museum of Art, New York; The Elisha Whittelsey Fund, 1968*)

22. Illustration of a bed with hangings and a wash table from Kimbel, *Journal für Möbelschreiner,* plate 3. (*The Metropolitan Museum of Art, New York; The Elisha Whittelsey Fund, 1968*)

23. Armchair, walnut, gilded. French. Eighteenth century. (*The Metropolitan Museum of Art, New York: Gift of J. Pierpont Morgan, 1906*)

did not render it realistically. The difference can be seen even more clearly by looking at an eighteenth-century engraving. English eighteenth-century furniture design publications suggest the same subtle generalizing. See the table (fig. 24) engraved by Thomas Langley in B. and T. Langley, *The City and Country Builder's and Workman's Treasury of Designs* ([London, 1740], plate CXLI).

One element that requires further study is the persistence of the rococo style. In provincial areas on the Continent the rococo never disappeared entirely. Although it was executed with great restraint so that it bears little resemblance to work in the revival style, there is a possibility that rococo techniques were learned from the *retardataire* craftsmen.

Because Belter is best known for his use of laminated wood, it is important to consider the technical background he acquired as an apprentice in Ulm, even though we can only theorize. As the second largest city in Württemberg, Ulm was doubtlessly a center of fashion. In the 1820s and 1830s that meant furniture makers would have favored the use of rosewood for furniture in the classical designs of the German Empire style called Biedermeier. At the time more provincial cabinetmakers worked in oak and local fruitwoods. Laminated pieces of wood that were made by gluing layers of veneers together were employed by cabinetmakers for ornamental details on Biedermeier pieces because they were stronger than plain pieces of solid wood. The technique had been used in the eighteenth century for brackets and fretwork that required extra curves or par-

24. Illustration of a marble table from B. and T. Langley, *The City and Country Builder's and Workman's Treasury of Designs* (London, 1740), plate CXLI.

ticular delicacy. It was not used for chairbacks or drawer sides as in the nineteenth century. Belter used laminated wood to create shapes that required elaborate bending operations involving the employment of molds or cauls. Bending solid wood was a familiar technique in the eighteenth century, and the caul is defined in Thomas Sheraton's *Cabinet Dictionary* (London: W. Smith, 1803), which is evidence that it was used to shape furniture prior to 1800.

It is very likely more than coincidental that laminated wood was used by Michael Thonet, another German innovator of the nineteenth century. Famous as the founder of the company that has made bentwood chairs since the 1830s, Thonet had grown up in Boppard, some 260 kilometers (161.46 mi) from Ulm, as the crow flies. He had used laminated wood for his first bentwood chairs. In both cases the motivation for using laminated wood was that it facilitated improvements in design and production techniques. Thonet's objective was an essentially functional line of furniture, whereas Belter strove to achieve a special elegance through the use of elaborate ornament. Both found that laminated woods were particularly strong and good for bending into curved shapes. The purely functional furniture conceived by Thonet was used in royal palaces before it became the standard café furnishing, whereas Belter's designs were meant for the homes of the newly affluent in the New World. After a few years Thonet went on to use a bent wood that was not laminated, and Belter developed a method of laminating that has been compared to plywood, but he must have been familiar with laminating techniques when he left for the New World.

Belter's first American efforts are not documented, but his success is evident in the fact that he moved from Chatham Street to a more fashionable location at 372 Broadway in 1846, only two years after he established his business. A year after the move he obtained a patent for "Machinery for Sawing Arabesque Chairs," dated July 31, 1847 (No. 5,208). The specifications describe a process using a single saw to cut out a chairback before it was attached to the chair or carved. Whether the wood was solid or laminated is not explained because the procedure would have been the same in either case. The reader of the patent is left to wonder about the embellishments to follow and how this chairback differed from the designs of other examples with pierced-work frames like the chair that appears in the Henkels' advertisement described earlier.

Dating Belter is not easy because there is evidence that many designs were used over a long period. One parlor set that seems to have disappeared was described as the documented work of the 1840s in a letter to Joseph Downs in 1948. It had been made for Governor Buckingham of Connecticut and was in the possession of a Mr. Cleary of Norwich when the letter was written, but until it is located we have no way of knowing the nature of its decoration. That the decoraion follows no set evolution from elaborate to simple, or vice versa, is suggested. Chairs in the Manney Collection containing newspaper fragments that suggest they were made between about 1849 and 1850 are pierced and carved in an elaborate oak, leaf, grape, and flower pattern related to examples in the parlor set that was purchased from Belter in 1851 by Tuthill King of Chicago. Examples with similar decoration were made later.

In 1852 the shop was moved farther uptown to 547 Broadway. A table at The Newark Museum with the unmistakable leaf and floral pattern by Belter on the skirt bears a label with the 547 Broadway address, but the cabinetmaker's name is missing from it. It was while the shop was at 547 that Belter exhibited the ebony and ivory center table at the New York Crystal Palace. It was also when the shop was at that location that listings in the directories changed from "John H. Belter, cabinet maker" to "John H. Belter, manufacturer." The change is found in the 1853 exhibition catalogue, although it was not until 1854 that the factory at Third Avenue and 76th Street was opened. The characterization of Belter as a manufacturer implied a change in the nature of the operation. Many of the same designs were made both before and after the expansion. One of the few parlor sets for which the original bill has survived, that purchased by Colonel B. S. Jordan of Milledgeville, Georgia, in 1855, is one of the most elegant examples of Belter's work and even more elaborate than the Tuthill King set made a few years before.

In 1856 the showrooms moved from 547 to 552 Broadway. It was also the year in which Belter obtained a patent (No. 15,552) for making a bedstead. Included in the specification is a description of a method of making laminated wood and bending it into the appropriate shapes. In his statement he said,

> I am aware that veneers glued together with the grain of each layer standing at right angles to the next have been long in use for the purpose of combining strength and lightness . . . What I claim as my invention and desire to secure by Letters Patent is a bedstead constructed of thin parts.

He also claimed the device for putting the bed together was patentable. Despite the disclaimers that the method of laminating and shaping was not original, the patent describes the technique at length so that it is helpful to the person trying to understand Belter's methods of construction. Belter stressed the fact that bending wood was common in his time. Throughout the application Belter insisted on the superiority of working with veneers over working with solid wood covered with a single layer of veneer. He explained that the finished product dried to be strong and serviceable enough for work done with ordinary tools, but advised gluing on "more wood to form a sufficient thickness for the carved portion when necessary."

Also at 552 Broadway, Belter's location after 1856, J. H. Springmeyer is listed as a furniture dealer. Springmeyer was Belter's brother-in-law, and he had two brothers, William and Fred, who were cabinetmakers working separately in the early 1850s who also were to join J.H. Belter & Co. Two labeled tables, one at the Museum of the City of New York, and the other in the Manney Collection, bear the 552 address. These tables are enough different from one another to provide further confirmation that working out a chronology for Belter is very challenging. Because one table is made of solid wood and the other is laminated, connoisseurs have evidence that Belter did not improve on his early work by introducing laminated wood. The major differences are in shape: the laminated table is round, and the solid table is rectangular. The scale of the ornament on each also differs, with the solid-wood table bearing ornament that is bolder and less delicate than the one made of veneers. Solid wood was practical for a table in a rectangular shape. The attributions cannot be questioned because they share the indisputable mark of the Belter shop in the quality and character of the carving. Belter motifs are carved with a convincing sense of realism that is very rare in the work of other shops. The Belter carvers captured a feeling that makes their flowers and leaves come alive, while most of the work of contemporary furniture carvers has the charm of the naïve artist-craftsman's work.

Belter obtained Patent No. 19,405 on February 23, 1958, which was titled "Improvement in the Method of Manufacturing Furniture," and is explained as "a new and useful Improvement in Pressed-Work Furniture . . ." The illustrations and the explanation concentrate on chairbacks, but Belter claimed, "My invention is not limited to the construction of chairbacks, but may be applied to all kinds of pressed-work furniture." He goes on to say, "My invention consists in giving increased beauty, strength, and other valuable qualities to what is termed 'pressed-work' furniture, by constructing it of two or more layers of pressed work staves." The use of staves is suggested as a replacement for the sheets of "pressed-work," or laminated wood, to make it possible to bend the wood into shapes that curve in more than one plane. Belter explained that the sheets could be bent in only one direction. The diagrams and the basic explanation involved making chairbacks. Eight were to be made at once as a barrellike unit in a simple caul and after they were dried, the unit would be sawed apart into the eight separate chairbacks. He referred to the shaping as *dishing,* and the drawings illustrate forms that are more elaborately shaped than most examples that are known, but the basic construcion was very likely used before 1858, as has been shown in chapter 3, "Technical Observations." Some patents were obtained years after a specific improvement was introduced. Belter was not alone in that. Thomas Blanchard of Boston had shown a machine for bending wood at the Mechanics Fair in Boston in 1850, but the patent he obtained for a wood-bending process is dated 1858.

Belter's fourth patent, dated January 24, 1860 (No. 26,881), was for "certain new and useful Improvements in Bureaus." There were four aspects to the patent. One dealt with the use of single sheets of pressed work for the drawers, and the other three were concerned with locking the bureau. The application provides further evidence of continual efforts to refine the processes of making what Belter called "pressed-work" furniture.

In 1861 the showrooms were moved to 722 Broadway. Belter's health failed in the course of the following two years and he died in 1863. His partners carried on the business until 1867 when it was closed after bankruptcy proceedings. A single bill for "blackwood chairs" dated 1864 shows that the Springmeyers continued to make Belter designs after his death, if we assume that the chair illustrated in "John Henry Belter and Company" by Joseph Downs, which appeared in The Magazine *Antiques* (54, no. 3 [September 1948], pp. 166–168), is the chair mentioned in the bill. A desk in the Manney Collection with the stenciled mark "Springmeyer Brothers, Successors to J.H. Belter and Company" is fine, relatively simple, but with rococo decoration. A bureau similarly marked in a private collection in Georgia is similarly restrained in the use of rococo detail.

The fact that the shop continued to be productive after his death would appear to be sufficient evidence that the myth of Belter's destruction of all his tools and designs when he was about to die cannot be corroborated. Besides that there is proof that in the settlement of affairs during the final proceedings Mrs. Belter purchased the machinery for ultimate resale because the auction price was too low.

John Henry Belter was an extraordinary figure in the history of American furniture. Although there is still a lot to be learned about him, evidence at hand proves he was the greatest furniture designer and manufacturer of the nineteenth century and, essentially, the man whose work was the bridge between eighteenth-century craftsmanship and nineteenth-century technology. That he worked in a single style, the Rococo Revival, is puzzling, but his career ended as it had begun, when the rococo was most in fashion.

THE ROCOCO REVIVAL STYLE AND THE WORK OF JOHN HENRY BELTER

Marvin D. Schwartz

John Henry Belter began working in New York when the Rococo Revival style first came into fashion. As we have seen, he had learned his craft in Württemberg where the rococo was introduced in the 1830s. On both sides of the Atlantic it was one of several styles that had come into fashion as a part of a new approach that involved revivals of early styles and the use of designs based on inspiration from historic sources. The Rococo Revival was the closest in time to its source. The most explicit American account of fashionable design at mid-century, Andrew Jackson Downing's *Architecture of Country Houses* (1850), enumerated the most popular historic sources as being Gothic, Norman, Elizabethan, Italian, French, and Grecian. Downing followed the precedent of English, French, and German writers in calling what we know as the rococo, *Louis Quatorze,* but he was not consistent, and he also called rococo designs *Louis XV*. Downing was probably reporting accurately when he wrote,

> *Modern French furniture,* and especially that in the style of *Louis Quatorze,* stands much higher in general estimation in this country than any other. Its union of lightness, elegance, and grace renders it especially the favorite of ladies . . . The style of Louis XIV is characterized by greater delicacy of foliage ornamentation and greater intricacy of detail. We may add to this, that besides the greater delicacy of foliage ornamentation and greater elegance of most French drawing-room furniture, its superior workmanship, and the luxurious ease of its admirably constructed seats, strongly commend it to popular favor. (p. 432)

American examples appear to have been made more extensively than those of European origin, as Downing observed. Certainly, it is the most elaborate of the popular revival styles. The rococo and the style Downing called Grecian, which is called Empire today, are the two that are best known in the period between 1840 and 1860. It was a period that was late for the Empire style, and examples of it are generally simple in line and without much carving. On the other hand, the rococo was the style of high fashion and was made in a variety of designs to suit a broad spectrum of taste as well as price. At the one extreme are the relatively simple designs that curved appropriately but had little ornament. At the other extreme are examples embellished with elaborate carving. The greater number of the elaborately decorated American examples appears to have been made in New York, but there are examples purchased in New Orleans that are almost as elaborate. Many may actually have been made in New Orleans, despite the fact that family histories frequently attribute their origins to Paris. The rich floral and fruit carving characteristic of the most elaborate work is not found on the French or Continental examples preserved in public collections in Europe. The designs called for curved frames for seating furniture and curved sides on chests and tables. These were made either by using traditional techniques to bend wood or by the more innovative method of making a special laminated wood by gluing veneers of wood together and pressing them into shape in a caul. In any case the forms were shaped with the curves exaggerated in comparison to eighteenth-century models. There appears to be a restrained version of the Rococo Revival style that was made all over the country. The Troy, New York, cabinetmakers, Galusha Brothers, produced work in designs not very different from those found in many parts of the country far from New York. A parlor set by Galusha at The Brooklyn Museum includes chairs in shapes that curve more boldly than basic eighteenth-century examples (fig. 25). Typical of handsomely made but restrained Rococo Revival furniture, the Brooklyn chairs have nicely molded rails and stiles with subtle carving in the crest rails. Downing recommended two cabinetmaking establishments where Rococo Revival furniture was available, Alexander Roux and Charles Platt, but he ignored John H. Belter who was making outstanding furniture by 1850, when *The Architecture of Country Houses* was published.

The furniture exhibited at the Crystal Palace ex-

25. Chair from a parlor set by Galusha Brothers, Troy, New York. (*The Brooklyn Museum, Brooklyn, New York*)

26. Sofa with a rosewood frame by Alexander Roux, New York. Illustrated in Benjamin Silliman and Charles Goodrich, *The World of Science, Art and Industry* (New York: G. P. Putnam & Co., 1854), p. 191.

27. Pier table with a rosewood frame and a white marble top by A. Eliaers, Cornhill, Boston. Illustrated in Silliman and Goodrich, *The World of Science,* p. 164.

28. Octagonal center table with a caryatid at each angle by Jules Dessoir, New York. Illustrated in Silliman and Goodrich, *The World of Science,* p. 175.

hibition held in New York in 1853 and 1854 showed that the Rococo Revival was one of the several fashionable styles of the period and illustrates a flamboyant aspect of work of the time. Officially titled "Industry of All Nations" (the same as the London Crystal Palace exhibition two years earlier), furniture exhibitors were attracted from many parts of Europe. *The World of Science, Art and Industry, Illustrated from Examples in the New York Exhibition, 1853–1854* (New York: G. P. Putnam & Co., 1854), which gives an account of the exhibition by Benjamin Silliman and Charles Rush Goodrich, offered a selection of the objects they deemed most important. As we know, J. H. Belter's contribution was ignored. The work included is consistently elaborate, as if the exhibitors were determined to show a complete lack of aesthetic restraint. For a furniture maker like the New York firm of Alexander Roux, the examples illustrate their most elegant efforts, but labeled furniture that has been located in recent years proves Roux made a broad range of furniture that included simple as well as elaborate work (fig. 26).

Most of the Rococo Revival pieces illustrated are based on designs conceived by combining eighteenth-century models and new shapes. The pier table by A. Eliaers of Boston, a furniture maker best known for his patented library chair, is a perfect example of the use of eighteenth-century rococo motifs rendered in high relief (or drawn for the engraving in a precise line that suggests high relief) to suit nineteenth-century taste (fig. 27). The center table by Jules Dessoir of New York was conceived as a brilliant display piece (fig. 28). Its octagonal top is supported by caryatids, which function as the ends of leaf-carved scroll legs that are rococo in spirit. Animals, flowers, and birds are among the motifs that make this piece more complex than the examples based on an eighteenth-century prototype. The sofa by Alexander Roux follows a basic eighteenth-century design, and its decoration is also rendered in more precise detail. The birds on the back would have been an unusual motif on the rococo prototype, and it was very likely taken from a Louis XIV design. Several chairs such as the one made by G. Zora of Turin are rococo in decoration and Louis XIV in overall design. The Rococo Revival examples at the New York Crystal Palace illustrated the popularity of the style and how it related to eighteenth-century design. They suggested that ornate examples were made in many places. It is amazing that none of the Rococo Revival examples illustrated resembled the typical products of the New York cabinetmakers who produced furniture in laminated woods.

The designs already mentioned in Downing's *Architecture of Country Houses* and those in the English, German, and American books published in the period between 1830 and 1860 are in the main quite different from those employed by Belter and the others. The books illustrate examples that are closer to the eighteenth-century models. While the eighteenth-century shapes were transformed to the scale preferred in the nineteenth century, the ornament revealed the obvious link to the original style. It is clear that the nineteenth-century designs were intended as adaptations rather than as reproductions of the rococo—reproductions were not popular until later in the century. As is evident in the illustrations of Crystal Palace examples, the more typical nineteenth-century examples by cabinetmakers working on both sides of the Atlantic differ from the eighteenth-century versions of rococo furniture in both form and detail. The nineteenth-century designer exaggerated the curves and made the details intricate. The leaf, shell, or flower is defined more precisely in the nineteenth-century work, which is to say that the masterful eighteenth-century manner of capturing the essence of a motif with a minimum of detail was replaced in the nineteenth century by rendering details with a greater realism, or, at least, in higher relief. The demands of nineteenth-century taste were met in different ways, depending on the approach of the carver. Some, like those working in the Belter shops, achieved a convincing realism in their rendering. Others stylized the same motifs that Belter used to achieve the three-dimensional counterpart of folk designs used in theorems blocked out on velvet, and still others, attempting to keep closer to the eighteenth-century models, rendered the early motifs on a bolder scale.

Most illustrations of Rococo Revival models in the design books by such authors or publishers as the English Thomas King and Henry Whitaker and the German Wilhelm Kimbel reflect the last approach and were conservatively conceived. The eighteenth-century motifs in their publications are rendered with much greater precision than in eighteenth-century engravings. In the work of Belter there is a more dramatic change, not only are the motifs rendered more realistically but their character is different. In the Belter examples the vocabulary of ornament is extensive. A variety of flowers, fruit, and vegetables is most prevalent, but cherubs (putti), birds, and shells are also found. The eighteenth-century vocabulary of ornament is more limited because the motifs are rendered in less detail. Construction is also an important factor. The use of laminated woods enabled the Belter shop to produce more fanciful shapes than those used in the eighteenth century or by the more conservative cabinetmakers of the nineteenth century.

As we have seen, the basic designs of furniture attributed to John Henry Belter are distinctive but not unique. Also, the technique of using the laminated woods he called "pressed-work" in designs of naturalistic ornament is found in work by other cabinetmakers.

29. Engraving after Jean-Baptiste Monnoyer. (*The Metropolitan Museum of Art, New York; Rogers Fund, 1920*)

30. Engraving after Jean Lepautre.

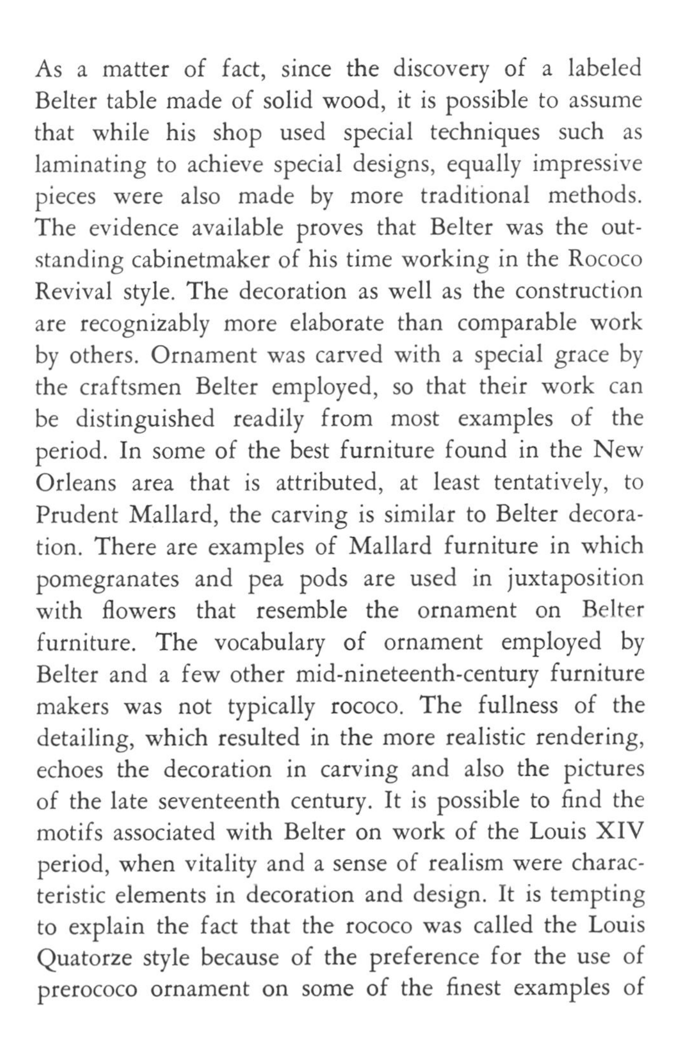

As a matter of fact, since the discovery of a labeled Belter table made of solid wood, it is possible to assume that while his shop used special techniques such as laminating to achieve special designs, equally impressive pieces were also made by more traditional methods. The evidence available proves that Belter was the outstanding cabinetmaker of his time working in the Rococo Revival style. The decoration as well as the construction are recognizably more elaborate than comparable work by others. Ornament was carved with a special grace by the craftsmen Belter employed, so that their work can be distinguished readily from most examples of the period. In some of the best furniture found in the New Orleans area that is attributed, at least tentatively, to Prudent Mallard, the carving is similar to Belter decoration. There are examples of Mallard furniture in which pomegranates and pea pods are used in juxtaposition with flowers that resemble the ornament on Belter furniture. The vocabulary of ornament employed by Belter and a few other mid-nineteenth-century furniture makers was not typically rococo. The fullness of the detailing, which resulted in the more realistic rendering, echoes the decoration in carving and also the pictures of the late seventeenth century. It is possible to find the motifs associated with Belter on work of the Louis XIV period, when vitality and a sense of realism were characteristic elements in decoration and design. It is tempting to explain the fact that the rococo was called the Louis Quatorze style because of the preference for the use of prerococo ornament on some of the finest examples of the Rococo Revival style. There is no evidence of specific connections, neither is there any way of proving that Belter and his contemporaries were particularly

31. Detail of a stairway at Cassiobury Park, Watford, Hertfordshire, by Grinling Gibbons. (*The Metropolitan Museum of Art, New York; Rogers Fund, 1932*)

conscious of late seventeenth-century art, save in the naming of the style. However, there is evidence of nineteenth-century republications of the early designs.

Prints of floral designs by Jean-Baptiste Monnoyer (1634–1699) and architectural projects by Jean Lepautre (1618–1682), both significant figures in the late seventeenth century, were available in reprints of the mid-nineteenth century and both could have been the inspiration for Belter ornament (figs. 29, 30). The distinctive characteristics of late seventeenth-century decoration—realism and clarity in rendering—are equally significant in the Belter ornament. Comparisons between Belter and late seventeenth-century work can be carried further. At the time of Louis XIV realism in ornament was a characteristic that was international. It was also to be found in the marvelous carvings by Grinling Gibbons, the English carver and sculptor who flourished from around 1670 to 1721. At The Metropolitan Museum of Art a stairway (fig. 31) from Cassiobury Park, Watford, Hertfordshire, by Gibbons provides an illustration of motifs rendered in a way that was to be inspirational for Belter. At Petworth, a country house with paneled walls embellished by Gibbons's carving, there are flowers and cherub heads; and there are birds at another house, Burghley, to name additional sources of motifs by Gibbons that were later favored by Belter. Although it is not possible to prove any direct connection, the comparisons prove a similarity in the taste of the two eras. The work of Gibbons epitomized decoration in the late seventeenth-century spirit. Gibbons's ornament was used for other objects to a lesser degree but was the inspiration for papier-mâché ornament manufactured by "Mr. Bielefeld of London" and illustrated on page 61 of the *Art Journal Catalogue* of the "Industry of All Nations" 1851 exhibition (better known as the Great Exhibition at the London Crystal Palace).

Although the obvious visual connection between the Belter ornament and Louis XIV sources may be a reason for the use of the name *Louis XIV* in references to rococo design, it is also possible that the mid-nineteenth century's conception of eighteenth-century style was less precise than today's. Craftsmen combining adaptations of eighteenth-century forms with ornament based on late seventeenth-century decoration may have considered the two sources contemporary.

The use of the late seventeenth-century ornament that was characteristic of Belter's production was not common on the work of the other furniture manufacturers who used laminated woods. This means that, in differentiating between work by Belter and furniture of laminated wood by contemporaries, the nature of the ornament is as important a distinguishing factor as the construction. In chapter 3 technical details such as the width and number of veneers have been shown to be a distinctive sign of work by Belter. The examples by other manufacturers were made of thicker veneers used more sparingly. There was a definite connection between the character of the decoration and the thickness of the veneers. The group of more finely made examples relate to documented work by Belter and were decorated with more elaborately executed ornament. The Belter-like furniture attributed to J. and J.W. Meeks bears a simpler kind of decoration than the documented work by Belter. The motifs in Meeks's pierced work on chairbacks and table skirts are flowers and scrolls or grapes and leaves that are rendered with less intricacy than decoration by Belter. Some decoration is based on eighteenth-century prototypes, but the carving on the cabriole legs of center tables appears to have been based on the Belter models, with leaves, roses, and other flowers rendered more schematically by Meeks.

The tendency to divide the output of Rococo Revival furniture into work that is made of laminated wood and that made of solid wood should be questioned. Belter's output falls into both categories, and if we accept the attribution of the examples made of laminated wood, Meeks's output also falls into the two categories, as would the work of Herter, Henkels, and others. The significant gauge of quality to be applied is the character of the design. Elegant furniture in the Rococo Revival style was conceived imaginatively, with subtle curves in the rococo spirit, and the carving was executed in high relief with the details precisely defined. The style was interpreted by cabinetmakers working on a number of levels, so there is a broad range from the elegant to examples made simply and with little or no ornament. Some of the simpler examples were made a decade or two after the style had gone out of fashion but they were also made along with the more elaborate examples in the 1850s. Simpler examples were made all over the country and have survived in quantity.

The Belter label said he made "All Kinds of Fine Furniture," although the furniture that has survived reveals a concentration on parlor sets. Nonetheless, hall, bedroom, dining room, and library pieces are known, if limited in quantity. One reason for all the parlor sets may be found in Downing who called the Rococo Revival style "the utmost luxury of decoration." He considered it to be most appropriate for the drawing room or for a lady's boudoir and better for use in a town house than in the country. In his account there were suggestions for a variety of styles that were to be used to set the right tone for each room. Because Downing's statement on interior decoration reflected an approach that was popular in the middle of the nineteenth century, rococo furniture like Belter's was deemed more important for the parlor than for other rooms. In 1850 the Renaissance Revival was beginning to be popular for dining rooms, and in many houses the Gothic was used for the entrance hall and the library. Two of the four patents Belter obtained were for bedroom pieces. He may have wanted to convince the public that the rococo could also be used attractively in bedrooms.

Dining room furniture by Belter is very rare, but the simple shield-back chairs have traditionally been called dining room chairs by a number of the families in which they have been owned. Although difficult to locate, dining tables with rococo ornament that may have been made by Belter are encountered occasionally. A few sideboards associated with Belter have been examined by Edward Stanek and Douglas True, and étagères with table-high central shelves could have been designed for use as dining room buffets. The cabinet or bookcase (plate 1) in the Manney Collection may well have been designed for a library, and it is possible that a fall-front desk with Rococo Revival ornament by Belter, like an example at the Museum of the City of New York by some other maker, may yet be found. One of the most extraordinary examples of work from the Belter factory is the hallstand in the Chrysler Museum at Norfolk, Virginia. This labeled piece must have been made for a house in which the entrance was done in the Rococo Revival style, an unexpected phenomenon because even the most elegant Southern mansions with rococo double parlors had either Elizabethan or Empire furnishings in their very grand entrance halls.

The output of the Belter shops between 1844 and 1867 would appear to have been limited to Rococo Revival designs in a relatively limited number of forms. While competitors like Roux, Meeks, and Herter produced furniture in a variety of styles, Belter concentrated on one. However, he used a variety of patterns in the single style. Dating the various patterns that were used is not easy. It would appear that a broad range of designs was available for most of the time the shops were productive. Defining the patterns for parlor furniture is challenging because there are few references to designs in contemporary documents, and there is impressive variety in the designs of surviving work. The juxtaposition of motifs and the subtle changes in the placement of details in pieces from a single set suggest that richness and almost infinite variety were objectives in the production of the parlor sets. The parlor furniture that had been used by the Vietor family, which included a labeled table at the Museum of the City of New York, has rich pierced-work borders that vary in detail from piece to piece.

Naming the patterns that were offered by Belter is difficult. The design books or catalogues that illustrated what was available from the Belter shops, once reported by members of the family to have survived, cannot be located. Only the bill for furniture for Colonel Jordan bears a reference to the pattern. Each of the items on the bill to Colonel Benjamin Smith Jordan, dated September 1855, is described as "ara-basket." Collectors have named other patterns for key pieces or sets that they know. The Jordan set and the Vietor set have elegantly carved, elaborate floral designs in which cornucopias are featured. The set for the Tuthill King family of Chicago, now in the Chicago Historical Society, has scrolls in place of the cornucopias and relates to several examples in the Manney Collection, but the Manney examples include even more variations on the basic pierced-work theme. Although the pierced decoration is used for the most elaborate designs, it was also popular for relatively early examples. The Kings acquired their set in 1851, according to family history. The Vietors owned bedroom furniture that was very likely acquired at the same time as the parlor furniture, and the bedroom bureau must have been made before 1861 when Belter obtained a patent for using a special technique to curve the sides of drawers, and one for a special locking device. Chairs closely related to examples in the King set have been discovered with fragments of newspaper on the inner surfaces under the upholstery. The dates on the newspapers are from the year 1849, which suggests that the King design had been familiar for a few years by the time it was ordered.

One of the most popular patterns for parlor furniture is relatively simple. Instead of piercing it has a plain curving molding to frame the upholstered sections of the backs of sofas and chairs, which is topped by a cresting of flowers and fruit. The cresting is sometimes made of a piece of wood applied to the back of the top rail and it projects in the back. As a kind of decorative filler between the upholstered section and the outer framing there is a group of inscribed parallel lines with dots between them on most examples of this pattern. According to family tradition, the key set in the design was acquired for Rosalie, one of the finest houses in Natchez, Mississippi, in 1859 or 1860, so the pattern is called Rosalie.

A more elaborate variation of the design, without pierced decoration, is one in which the solid back has a ribbon or shell motif carved to serve as an inner border between the upholstered back and the curving molding. It has a decorative cresting like the Rosalie set. The key set is found at Ashland just outside of Lexington, Kentucky, and as the house was Henry Clay's home, the furniture pattern is called Henry Clay or Clay.

Just about all of the Belter parlor furniture has elegant carving on the legs. A few examples have plain molded legs, but more examples with cabriole legs have floral motifs carved on the legs and the skirt. Again, there is amazing variety in the decoration on the legs, but there is a consistency in the fact that the patterns employed by Belter are in the main elaborate and realistic, whereas the work of his competitors is apt to have more stylized embellishments. A cartouche is frequently found on the skirt of work attributed to Meeks, but occasionally a Meeks chair will have a flower that is more simply rendered than those on the Belter examples. The Belter examples vary in the scale of the ornament and in the motifs employed, but there is never decoration that is in any way crude on these examples.

In going over the designs employed by Belter, the most impressive factor is the richness of the detailing of the typical work. Although a lot of furniture by Belter was made of laminated wood, there have been notable exceptions, including one labeled table. Belter furniture reflects a knowing virtuosity that distinguishes it from almost everything made at the time, and it is not easy to forget the statement found in the notes of Dun (predecessors to Dun and Bradstreet) in March 1860, when they stated that Belter "Makes first rate work, too gd to be profit." Clearly, Belter mastered the Rococo Revival style and produced the finest interpretations of it by introducing new techniques to shape furniture that was to be carved as elegantly as anything made in New York at the time.

A GALLERY OF FURNITURE FROM THE COLLECTION OF GLORIA AND RICHARD MANNEY

Compiled and arranged by
Marvin D. Schwartz, Edward J. Stanek, and Douglas K. True

The Manney furniture collection, with its focus on the work of John Henry Belter, illustrates the scope of New York's most important mid-nineteenth-century cabinetmaker, who was active from 1840 to 1863. Although Mr. and Mrs. Manney realize their collection is still growing, they feel that publishing and exhibiting it at this point is warranted because this selection of examples will enable students to learn the basic characteristics of the furniture Belter produced. Once the style is better known, and more connoisseurs are capable of distinguishing the output of Belter, it should be possible to discover forms that are unknown today but that must have been part of the Belter factory production. Desks, dining room tables, sideboards, and armoires are forms that may turn up.

The descriptions of the objects listed in this gallery have included the motifs and, to some degree, the patterns employed by Belter. The innovative analysis of the construction of pieces made of laminated wood devised by Edward J. Stanek and Douglas K. True was employed to investigate details in construction and design. Stanek and True have been working on an investigation of the methods Belter used in the manufacture of furniture for some time, and their complete findings will be published in due course. They were kind enough to discuss their findings in chapter 3 and to make them available for this book. Their research proves that Belter's manufacturing techniques were as distinctive as the ornament on the furniture he made. They have made it clear that there is a direct relation between the character of the ornament and the ways pieces were laminated.

The upholstery on the Manney furniture is modern, but the fabrics selected by Mrs. Manney are appropriate and in the spirit of the Rococo Revival. Silks and velvets were favored for elegant Rococo Revival furniture in the middle of the nineteenth century, although contemporary records list horsehair, wools, plush, and leather as other materials that were used. Tufted seats and backs were frequently used, although there are examples of the period that were made without tufting. Designs in which floral patterns were featured, often based on eighteenth-century models, were most popular. These were made of silk in monochrome damasks and polychrome brocades and brocatelles with more intricate designs and often stronger colors than in the eighteenth-century versions. Velvets of the period appear to have been inspired by late seventeenth-century (or Louis XIV) models. Nineteenth-century colors varied greatly but tended to be brighter than those used on earlier examples.

This gallery is intended to be a survey of furniture by John Henry Belter, and it includes a few examples by his contemporaries to help heighten the reader's perception and understanding of the work of one of the most significant figures in the history of American furniture. Dating has been omitted because, for now, we find that Belter furniture produced between around 1847 and 1865 is consistent in form, ornament, and spirit.

2. Armchair, rosewood with laminated back (7 layers of veneers). H. 38¾", W. 22", D. 21". Small or "lady's" chair with the back bent into the arc of a circle. The chairback is enclosed by an ovolo molding with scrolls to accent the bottom and top sections. Horizontal lines are inscribed in the upper area between the molding and the upholstery. The cresting is in a floral and fruit pattern resembling the ornament on the parlor set at Rosalie, Natchez, Mississippi. There are roses on the legs and skirt.

3 & 3a. Armchair, rosewood with laminated back (7 layers of veneers). H. 43", W. 22", D. 21". A larger, "gentleman's" chair in a design matching the chair in plate 2.

1. Bookcase or cabinet, glass, rosewood and maple veneers. H. 92½", W. 58", D. 22½". Rectangular in shape with glazed doors and sides enclosing an area backed with maple veneer and with maple-veneer shelves. It is topped by an elaborately carved pediment pierced in an elegantly detailed, leafy scroll pattern.

4, 4a, & 4b. Armchair, rosewood with laminated back (7 layers of veneers). H. 27½", W. 14", D. 12½". A miniature or child's armchair in a design matching the chair in plate 3, but the back (4a) is made as a separate piece attached to the rear legs at the corners of the seat. The arm supports and knuckles (4b) are leaf-carved.

5, 5a, & 5b. Armchair, rosewood with laminated, pierced back (8 layers of veneers). H. 44", W. 23", D. 22". The back (5a) wraps around to the front legs and is upholstered with a pear-shaped cushion. The elaborate pierced-work ornament (5b) is a combination of cornucopia, leaf, and floral motifs. There are floral decorations on the skirt and knees.

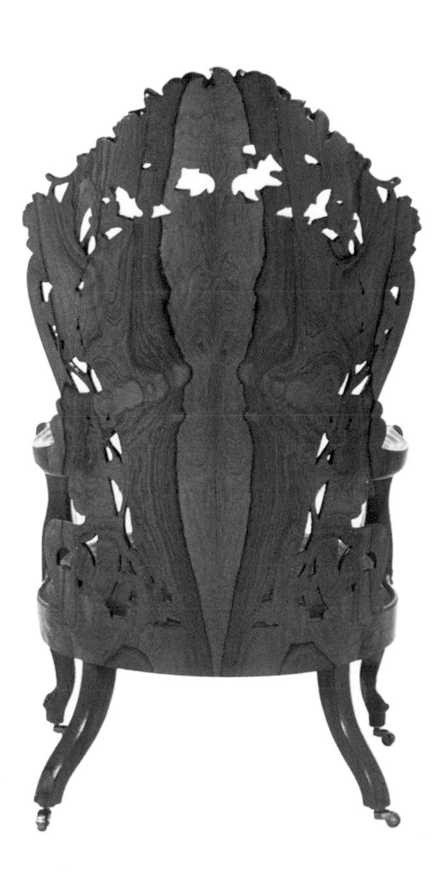

6 & 6a. Armchair, rosewood with laminated, pierced back (8 layers of veneers). H. 46″, W. 21½″, D. 21″. Large size with several unusual features. The piece is upholstered back and front with an open area between the back and the seat (6a), and a row of spindles is concealed by the upholstery but without finish. The arms terminate in lion's heads with two filled-in holes on the arms, which were probably made to hold the ends of a tray, making this a type of "reading chair." The pierced frame is decorated with a floral, fruit, and scroll design with cornucopias related to the decoration on the Tuthill King parlor set in the Chicago Historical Society. The front cabriole legs are unusually angled and elaborately shaped with a leaf design on the knees and skirt.

7. Armchair, rosewood with laminated back (8 layers of veneers). H. 45½″, W. 21″, D. 23½″. Unusually low arms that could be interpreted as bracing, and a pear-shaped back. The back veneers wrap around. The decoration consists of floral and fruit motifs with grapes crowning the cresting over scrolls. It is related to the Rosalie design. The front cabriole legs and the skirt are embellished with floral carving.

8. Armchair, rosewood with laminated, pierced back (8 layers of veneers). H. 40¼″, W. 23½″, D. 21″. Wide pierced-work border in a cornucopia, leaf, flower, and fruit pattern. The crest crowning the back is carved from an applied piece of wood. The skirt and the cabriole legs are carved in a continuous pattern. The back wraps around.

9 & 9a. Armchair, rosewood with laminated, pierced back (7 layers of veneers). H. 47½", W. 20½" D. 23". The back curves unusually with an accentuated cresting topped by floral and urn carving on an extra-thick piece of wood that has been applied. The decoration of the pierced-work border is a grape and leaf design with a cornucopia at the break between the upper and lower sections of the upholstery. The border continues to the front arm support (9a), as does the back cushion. The grape and floral carving on the cabriole legs and skirt is continuous.

10. Armchair (one of a pair), rosewood with laminated back (7 layers of veneers). H. 42¼", W. 25¼", D. 22". Kidney-bean-shaped back framed with a solid decorative border consisting of a double-scroll molding enclosing a strip of ribbed-shell motif surrounding the back cushion. The cresting is carved in floral and fruit motifs. There are roses at the knees of the front cabriole legs and a leaf pattern in the center of the skirt. Related to the set at Ashland, Henry Clay's home in Lexington, Kentucky.

11 & 11a. Armchair, rosewood with laminated back (7 layers of veneers). H. 39¼″, W. 22½″, D. 20½″. A simple shield-back chair topped by a cresting in a carved floral design, thickened by the addition of a piece of wood to the back (11a). The plain curving arms and the simplicity of the cabriole legs argue for this having been used as a dining chair.

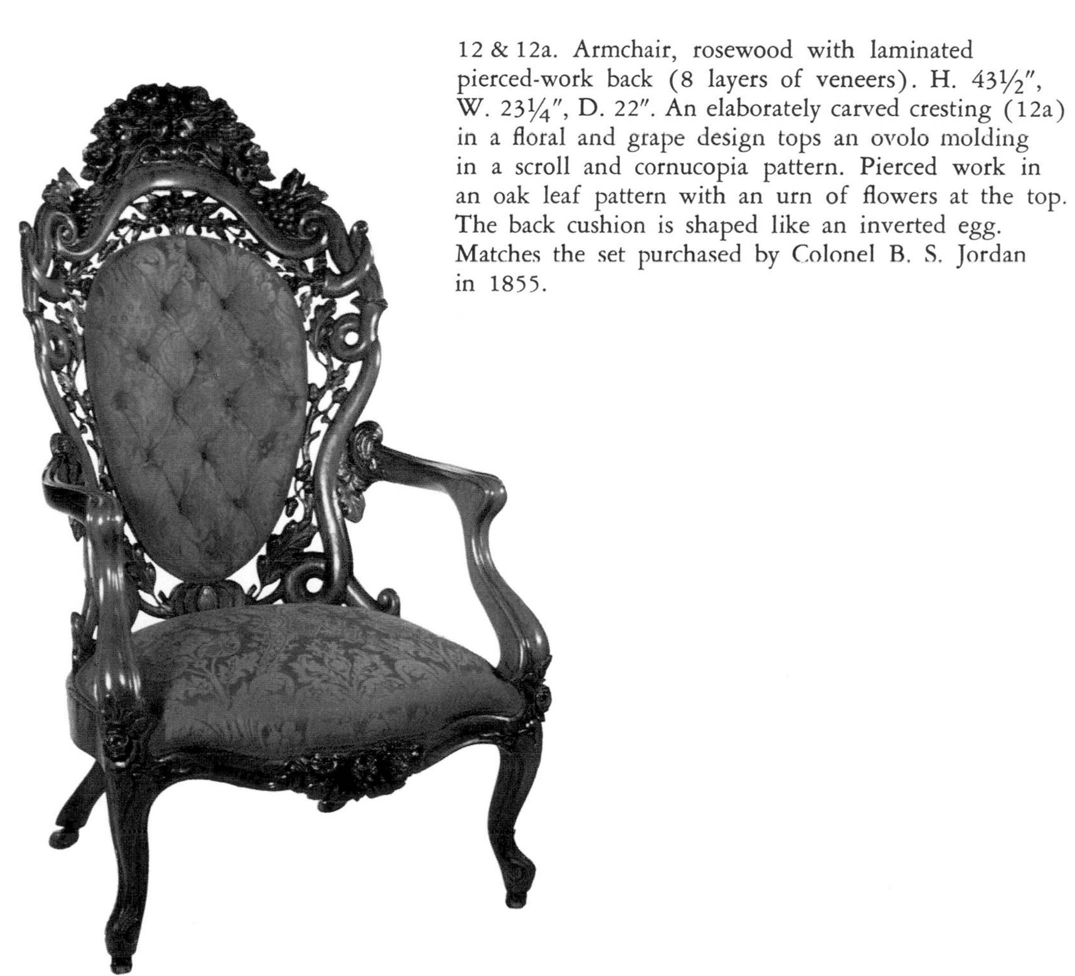

12 & 12a. Armchair, rosewood with laminated pierced-work back (8 layers of veneers). H. 43½″, W. 23¼″, D. 22″. An elaborately carved cresting (12a) in a floral and grape design tops an ovolo molding in a scroll and cornucopia pattern. Pierced work in an oak leaf pattern with an urn of flowers at the top. The back cushion is shaped like an inverted egg. Matches the set purchased by Colonel B. S. Jordan in 1855.

13, 13a, & 13 b. Side chair, rosewood with laminated back (7 layers of veneers). H. 38½″, W. 18″, D. 18″. A round seat on straight columnar legs that are round in cross section, topped by Corinthian capitals (13a). The back (13b) is a border of plain molding in a scroll design topped by the head of a bearded male in a skullcap, which is probably a portrait of Shakespeare. Part of a set.

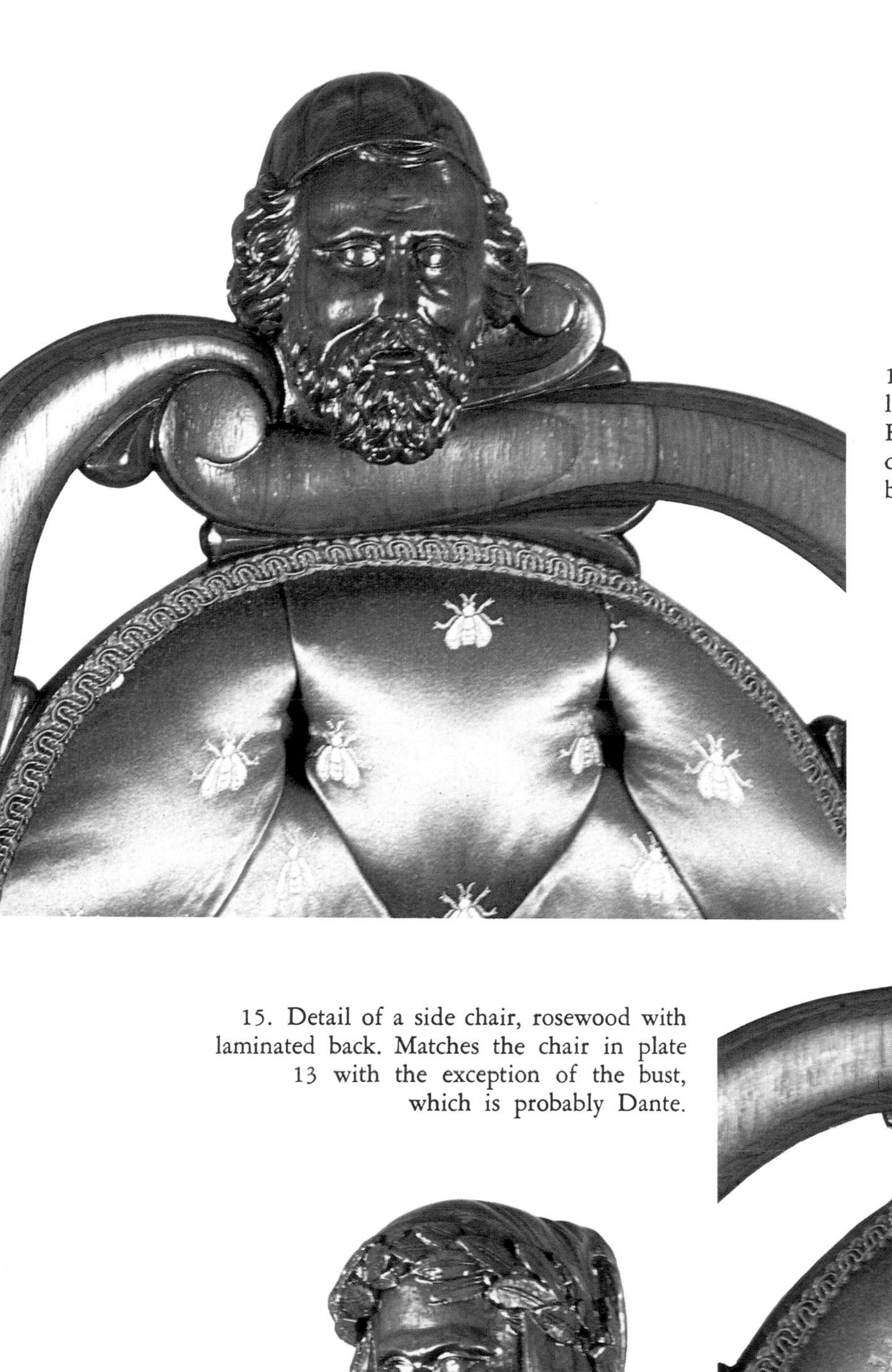

14. Detail of a side chair, rosewood with laminated back (7 layers of veneers). H. 38½", W. 18", D. 18". Matches the chair in plate 13 with the exception of the bust, which is probably Chaucer.

15. Detail of a side chair, rosewood with laminated back. Matches the chair in plate 13 with the exception of the bust, which is probably Dante.

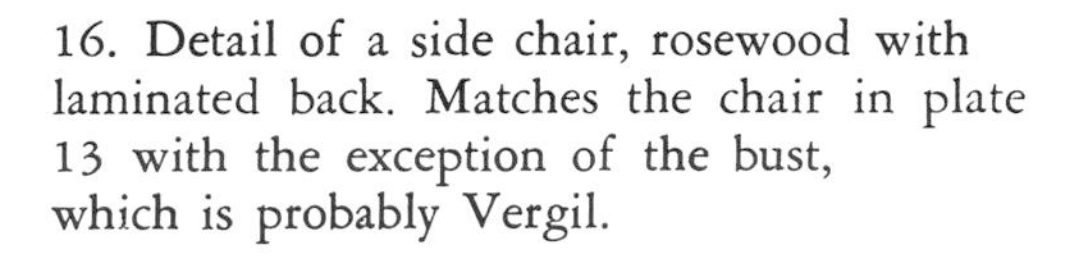

16. Detail of a side chair, rosewood with laminated back. Matches the chair in plate 13 with the exception of the bust, which is probably Vergil.

17. Side chair, rosewood with laminated, pierced back (8 layers of veneers). H. 32″, W. 16½″, D. 16½″. The back is not upholstered and has two thicknesses of pierced work in pressed wood. Most of the back is pierced in intricate, flat, leaf designs. In the center is an oval medallion with a grape and leaf design in relief. Simple cabriole legs. This may have been used at a dressing table.

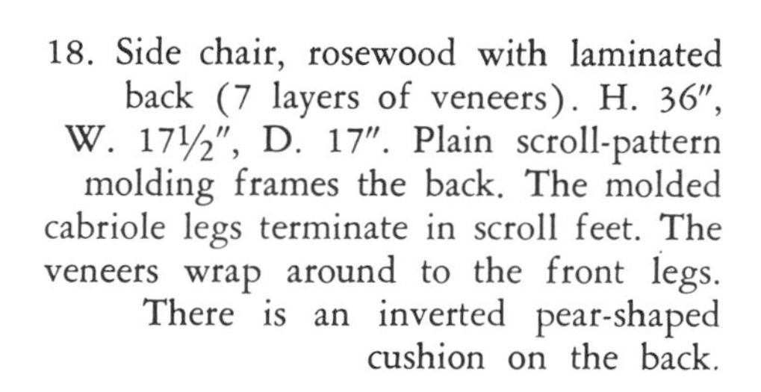

18. Side chair, rosewood with laminated back (7 layers of veneers). H. 36″, W. 17½″, D. 17″. Plain scroll-pattern molding frames the back. The molded cabriole legs terminate in scroll feet. The veneers wrap around to the front legs. There is an inverted pear-shaped cushion on the back.

19 & 19a. Side chair, rosewood with laminated, pierced back (6 layers of veneers plus one thick sheet). H. 36¼″, W. 19½″, D. 19½″. An elaborate floral leaf and acorn design is enclosed by a molded border embellished with scrolls and cornucopias. The top cresting is on an applied piece covered with a layer of veneer on the back (19a). Flowers at the knees of the front cabriole legs and in the center of the skirt. The curve is exaggerated.

20 & 20a. Side chair, rosewood with laminated back (7 layers of veneers). H. 37″, W. 18½″, D. 18″. The back (20a) is almost cabochon-shaped with the characteristic decorative elements of the set at Ashland, Henry Clay's home in Lexington, Kentucky.

21 & 21a. Side chair (one of a pair), rosewood with laminated, pierced back (7 layers of veneers). H. 36½", W. 19", D. 17½". The pierced-work back (21a) has large-scale oak leaf and flowers enclosed by a border of moldings in scroll forms that curve elaborately. The back cushion is small and round. There are roses on the knees and a rose and a wild rose in the center of the skirt. The veneers wrap around. The fruit and flower cresting is carved on an applied piece.

22. Side chair, rosewood with laminated, pierced back (5 layers of veneers). H. 40″, W. 20″, D. 20″. Probably not by J. H. Belter. The first acquisition of a piece of "Belter furniture" by the Manneys, this chair is more elaborately ornamented than the so-called Meeks examples. The border molding is complex but the pierced ornament is part of a narrow border uncharacteristic for Belter and is in a relatively simple leaf design. There is an urn of flowers on the cresting. The rear legs are unusual in having scrolls at the juncture with the seat.

23. Side chair, oak with laminated, pierced back (7 layers of veneers). H. 38″, W. 18½″, D. 18″. The pierced back is in an interlace pattern with the fruit and leaves undulating in the manner of slipper chairs and is made separate and attached to the rear legs.

24 & 24a. Side chair (one of a pair), rosewood with laminated back (7 layers of veneers). H. 36½", W. 18½", D. 17½". Pierced-work border with large-scale oak leaf, acorn, and oak flower motifs enclosed by a border of molding made of a long and short scroll on each side topped by a center scroll with a floral crest carved on an applied piece. There are roses on the knees of the cabriole legs and across the front skirt. The egg-shaped area for upholstery on the back (24a) contains fragments of newspaper dated 1849.

25 & 25a. Slipper chair (one of a pair), rosewood with laminated back (7 layers of veneers). H. 44¼", W. 17½", D. 16½". Low seat with an undulating back attached to the seat at the rear legs (25a). The pierced work is carved in oak leaves and acorns, enclosed by a molding in a scroll and cornucopia design, crowned with a floral and fruit cresting. The cabriole legs have flowers at the knees. There is an oval cushion on the back.

26. Slipper chair, rosewood with laminated, pierced back (7 layers of veneers). H. 37¾", W. 18", D. 18". Square seat, with curving sides on cabriole legs with molded edges but no carving. The undulating back is all wood, made of a simple, broad ovolo molding crowned by a leaf-carved cresting. The back is attached to the seat at the rear legs.

27 & 27a. Slipper chair, rosewood with laminated back (7 layers of veneers). H. 37", W. 18½", D. 17". The shape and construction are similar to the chair in plate 26 but the undulating back has a center area (27a) elaborately carved in a grape, acorn, and leaf design. The chair is crowned by a floral and fruit crest. There are roses on the knees of the cabriole legs and in the center of the front skirt.

28. Slipper chair, rosewood with laminated back (7 layers of veneers). H. 37½″, W. 19″, D. 17″. Similar to the chair in plate 27, with decoration on the back consisting of pendant grapes and oak leaves.

29 & 29a. Slipper chair, rosewood with laminated, pierced back (7 layers of veneers). H. 43¼″, W. 18″, D. 17¼″. The undulating back (29a), attached to the rear legs, is upholstered with a long, narrow, oval cushion. The outer border consists of an ovolo molding in a cornucopia design in the lower section on either side and unusual scrolls on the top separated by a cabochon, holding grapes below the floral crest. Acorn and leaf design in the narrow pierced section. There are roses on the knees, flowers on the skirt.

30. Étagère, rosewood. H. 93″, W. 52½″, D. 13″. Four rows of small shelves flank an arched center mirror topped by an elaborate crest with a shield in the center to back the floral pendant. The shelf brackets are cut out in a scroll design. There is carved decoration on the center of the base in a shell and leaf design.

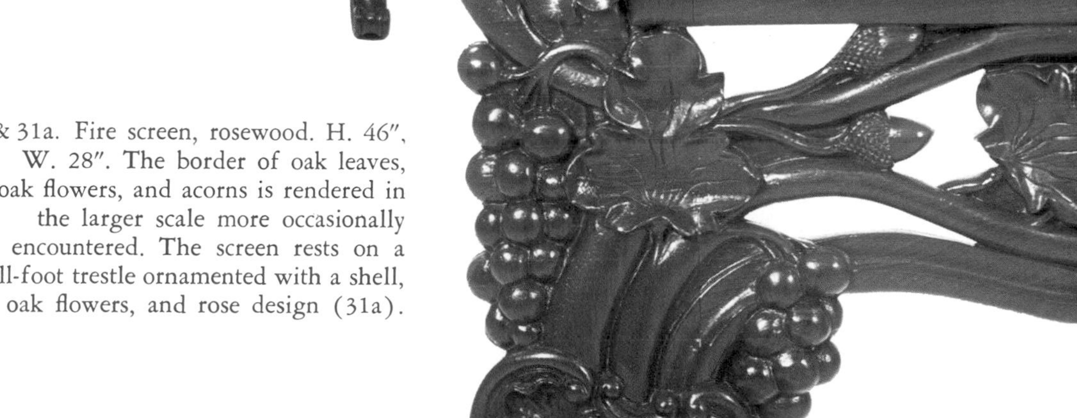

31 & 31a. Fire screen, rosewood. H. 46″, W. 28″. The border of oak leaves, oak flowers, and acorns is rendered in the larger scale more occasionally encountered. The screen rests on a scroll-foot trestle ornamented with a shell, oak flowers, and rose design (31a).

32. Sofa (one of a pair), rosewood with laminated back (7 layers of veneers). H. 35", W. 61", D. 32". A three-part curving frame with molded cabriole front legs terminating in leafy scroll feet. There are roses at the knees and in the center of the skirt. The arms curve in from the back and turn out at the ends. Each section is crowned by a cresting of flowers and fruit over a broad molding with a "filler" of incised lines and dots between the molding and the cushion in the manner of the parlor set at Rosalie, Natchez, Mississippi.

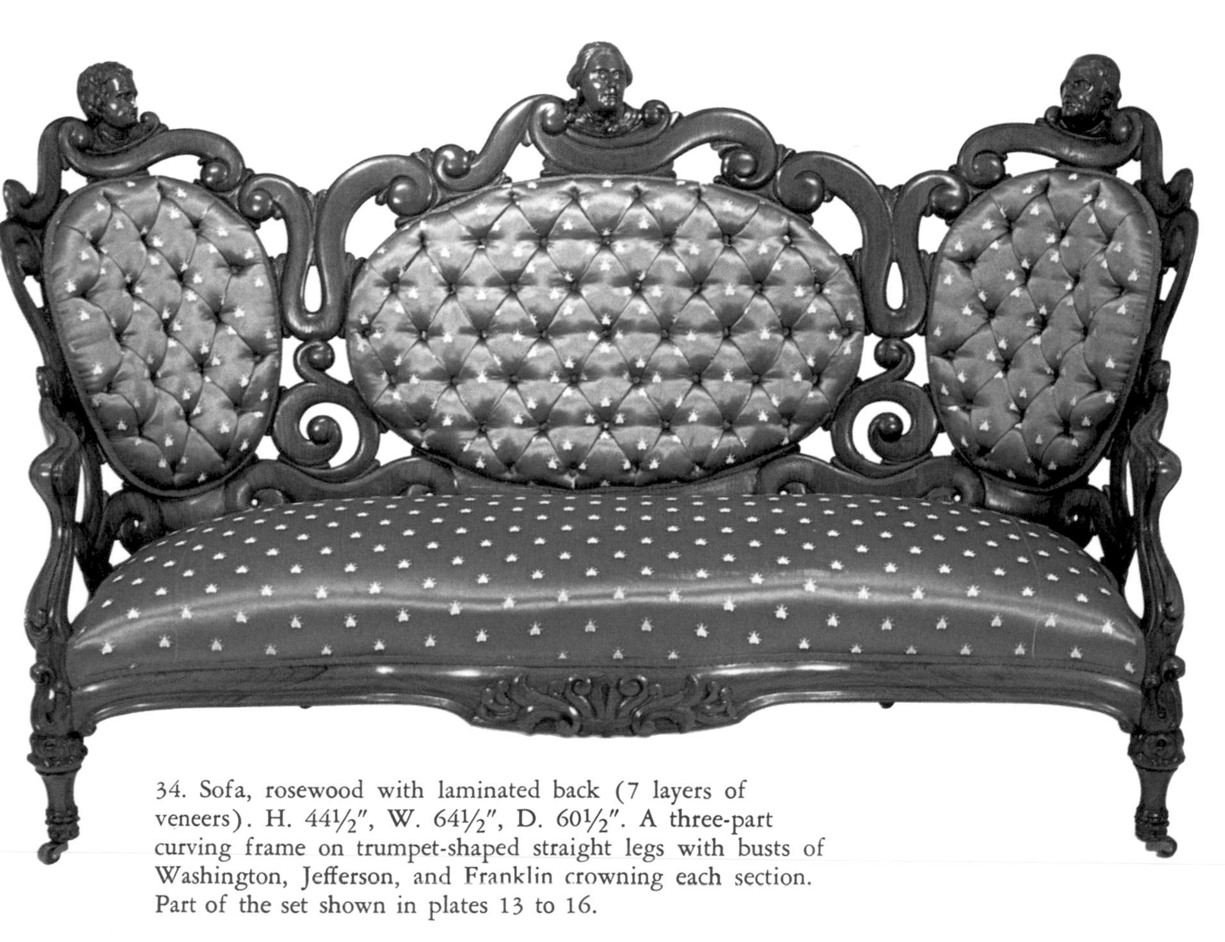

34. Sofa, rosewood with laminated back (7 layers of veneers). H. 44½", W. 64½", D. 60½". A three-part curving frame on trumpet-shaped straight legs with busts of Washington, Jefferson, and Franklin crowning each section. Part of the set shown in plates 13 to 16.

33 & 33a. Sofa, rosewood with laminated, pierced back (8 layers of veneers). H. 50¼″, W. 54½″, D. 25″. A three-part curving frame on molded front cabriole legs terminates in leafy scroll feet with rose and leaf carving at the knees and a rose and a petaled flower in the center of the skirt. The arms curve in from the back and turn out at the ends. Oak leaves and acorns are the dominant motifs of the pierced section with an ovolo molding in a cornucopia design on either side. The cresting (33a) of each section is carved in an elaborate floral and fruit design.

35 & 35a. Sofa, mahogany with laminated, pierced back (12 to 19 layers of veneers). H. 50″, W. 60¾″, D. 25″. A three-part curving frame on cabriole front legs terminates in leafy scroll feet with roses at the knees and more elaborate floral and leaf carving in the center of the skirt (35a). The pierced work consists of elaborate roses, oak leaves, and acorns. The cresting is carved in a particularly high-relief floral design and with grapes added to the sections at the left and right. The rear legs are unusual in that the top ends show through the skirt.

36. Sofa, rosewood with laminated back (7 layers of veneers). H. 41″, W. 55″, D. 25″. A three-part sofa with a border of ribbed shell between the outer strip of plain molding and the upholstery. Related to the set at Ashland, Henry Clay's home, Lexington, Kentucky.

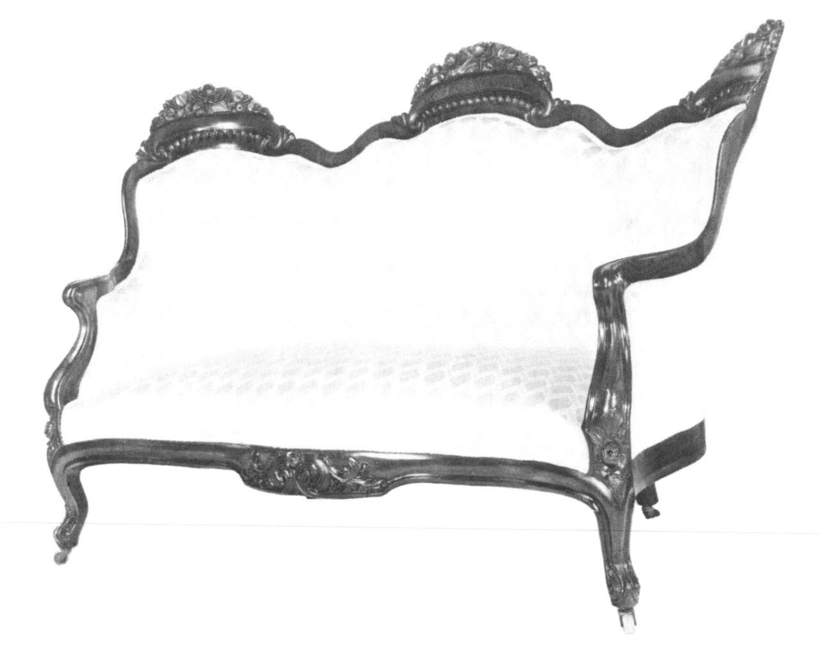

37 & 37a. Sofa, rosewood with laminated, pierced back (7 layers of veneers). H. 53″, W. 66″, D. 25″. A three-part frame elaborately carved with an undulating skirt. The pierced work at the top is in an urn, flower, and bird pattern (37a). The arms have protruding wood supports with spiral fluting, the center leg is in a high-relief floral design. The rear legs are unusual in being straight rather than canted out.

38. Sofa, rosewood with laminated back (8 layers of veneers). H. 42″, W. 63″, D. 33½″. A three-part curving frame on cabriole legs with floral decoration on the knees and across the skirt terminates in leafy scroll feet. There are flowers in the crests of each section, and fruit has been added on the sides and pea pods and grapes in the center. The rear legs are unusual in being straight, rather than canted out.

40. Méridienne (one of three), rosewood with laminated back (7 layers of veneers). H. 37″, W. 35″, D. 17½″. A curving frame crowned by an elaborate floral and fruit crest with a border of ribbed shell between the border molding and the upholstery in the manner of the Henry Clay set. The front cabriole legs have roses at the knees and carved flowers in the center of the skirt.

39, 39a, 39b. Sofa, oak with laminated back frame (7 layers of veneers). H. 53″, W. 66″, D. 25″. The frame is open rather than enclosed by a laminated back. Sea monsters like those found in table-leg designs flank an elaborate floral cresting (39a). There are lion's-head arm terminals and lion's-paw feet on the cabriole front legs (39b).

41. Méridienne, rosewood. H. 38¼", W. 36½", D. 23". Part of the set shown in plates 13 to 16 crowned by portrait busts, this one is of Milton.

42. Méridienne, rosewood. Matches the méridienne in plate 41 but this bust is of Shakespeare.

43. Piano stool, rosewood with laminated, pierced back (5 layers of veneers). H. 33½″, W. 15″, D. 15″. By a competitor of J. H. Belter. Round seat with a pierced-work back in a scroll pattern with a shield in the center in a star-and-stripes design. The seat rotates up and down on an urn-shaped base with four scroll legs.

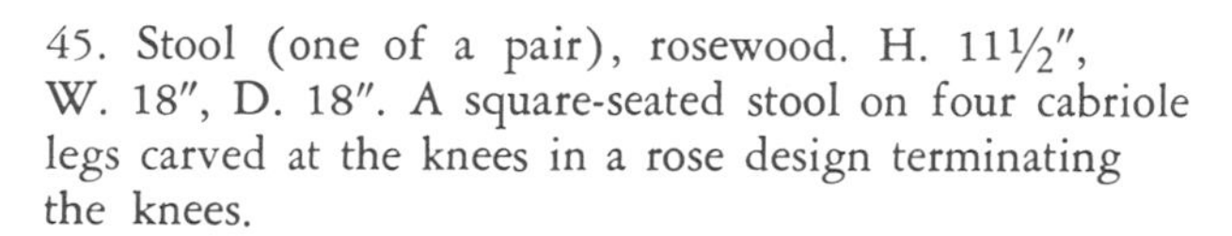

45. Stool (one of a pair), rosewood. H. 11½″, W. 18″, D. 18″. A square-seated stool on four cabriole legs carved at the knees in a rose design terminating the knees.

44. Piano stool, rosewood with laminated back (7 layers of veneers). H. 34½″, W. 14½″, D. 13″. A rectangular seat with an upholstered back in a design that relates to the set at Rosalie. The back is attached to the rear of the seat in the manner of a slipper chair. The seat rotates up and down on a leaf-decorated urn-shaped base with four scroll legs embellished with fruit.

46 & 46a. Table, center, rosewood with laminated, pierced skirt (10 layers of veneers). H. 28½″, Diam. 31″. A circular wooden top on four undercut cabriole legs carved at the knees in a rose design terminating in leafy scroll feet. The skirt motifs (46a) include leaves above each leg, and grapes, scrolls, and a cartouche in the center of each side. The stretchers cross to meet in the center and support an urn of roses, peonies, and possibly carnations in high relief.

47, 47a, 47b, & 47c. Table, center, rosewood with white marble top. H. 29″, W. 32″, L. 41″. A turtle-top on a solid skirt with a curving bottom edge. The skirt is decorated with applied leaf-and-scroll carving on the short sides and scroll-and-flower on the long sides in a design found on bureau-drawer pulls. The cabriole legs are in the shape of fantastic beasts (47a, 47b), (bird, dolphin, and horses), tails up, heads down, leaning on scrolls that are joined to the stretchers, which cross to support an urn filled with flowers, fruits, and vegetables (47c). Related to the tables at Rosalie.

48, 48a, & 48b. Table, center, rosewood with laminated, pierced skirt and white marble top (10 layers of veneers). H. 28¼″, W. 28″, L. 28¼″. A turtle-top on a pierced skirt is carved in a grape and vine pattern with an escutcheon in the center of each side carved in scroll, leaf, and floral design (48a). The undercut cabriole legs have flowers on the knees hanging down from leafy scrolls and terminate in leafy scroll feet. Thin scroll-shaped stretchers cross to support an urn of flowers (peonies, roses, and carnations) in naturalistic high relief (48b).

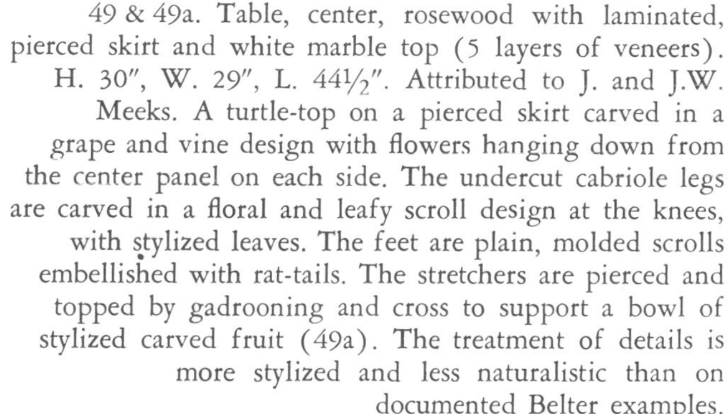

49 & 49a. Table, center, rosewood with laminated, pierced skirt and white marble top (5 layers of veneers). H. 30", W. 29", L. 44½". Attributed to J. and J.W. Meeks. A turtle-top on a pierced skirt carved in a grape and vine design with flowers hanging down from the center panel on each side. The undercut cabriole legs are carved in a floral and leafy scroll design at the knees, with stylized leaves. The feet are plain, molded scrolls embellished with rat-tails. The stretchers are pierced and topped by gadrooning and cross to support a bowl of stylized carved fruit (49a). The treatment of details is more stylized and less naturalistic than on documented Belter examples.

50 & 50a. Table, center, rosewood with laminated, pierced skirt and black and gray marble top (6 layers of veneers). H. 30½″, W. 28″, L. 45″. Attributed to J. and J.W. Meeks. Oval top on a skirt cut out in a scroll design with flowers on the panels in the center of each side. The undercut cabriole legs have leafy scrolls and pendant flowers at the knees and scroll feet. The stretchers consist of pierced work in a scroll design topped by a flat scroll border and cross to support a bowl of simply carved fruit (50a).

51. Table, center, rosewood with laminated, pierced skirt and white marble top. H. 29″, Diam. 30½″. A round table on on four cabriole legs with grapes and flowers on the knees. The legs terminate in leafy scroll feet. Simple scroll stretchers support a central urn of flowers with a turned turnip-shaped drop under it. The pierced skirt is carved in an oak leaf and acorn pattern with eagles in the center of each side.

52 & 52a. Table, center, ebony, ivory and white. H. 19½", Diam. 40¼" (cut off just above stretcher). The table "J. H. Belter, furniture manufacturer" that was exhibited at the New York Crystal Palace exhibition in 1853. A round top on a pierced-work skirt carved in a grape and vine design. (The ebony surface is so dark that it is not possible to see if there are layers of veneers.) The top parts of the legs are carved in an elaborate grape and flower design. There are ivory busts of Washington, Franklin, Jefferson, and Pierce (52a). The table was listed in the official catalogue but not mentioned in the illustrated publication.

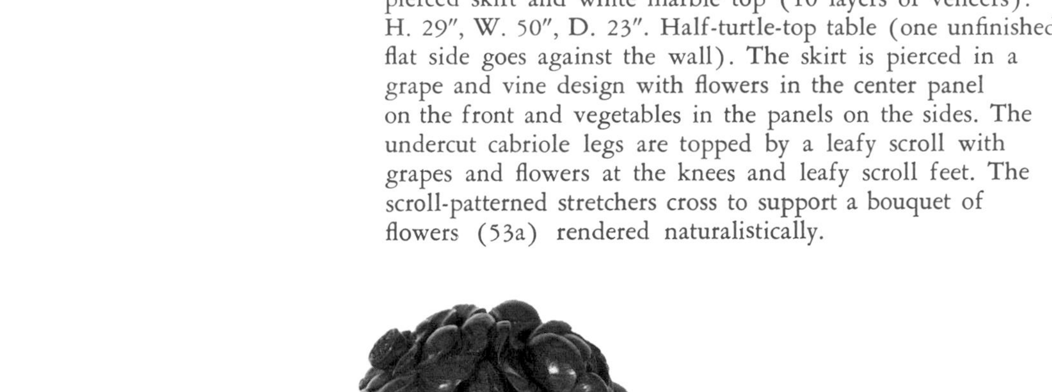

53 & 53a. Table, serving or console, rosewood with laminated, pierced skirt and white marble top (10 layers of veneers). H. 29″, W. 50″, D. 23″. Half-turtle-top table (one unfinished flat side goes against the wall). The skirt is pierced in a grape and vine design with flowers in the center panel on the front and vegetables in the panels on the sides. The undercut cabriole legs are topped by a leafy scroll with grapes and flowers at the knees and leafy scroll feet. The scroll-patterned stretchers cross to support a bouquet of flowers (53a) rendered naturalistically.

54, 54a, & 54b. Table, serving or console, rosewood with laminated, pierced skirt and white marble top (10 layers of veneers). H. 31″, W. 50″, D. 23″. This closely resembles the table in plate 53, with a difference in the decoration of the center panels on the skirt (54a) and on the casters (54b).

MANUFACTURERS OF
ALL KINDS OF FINE FURNITURE
NEW YORK.

◊ 55 & 55a. Table, library, rosewood with white marble top. H. 29″, W. 44″, D. 28″. Bears label (55a) with the address 552 Broadway. A rectangular form with scalloped sides on the skirt and the marble top. The solid-wood skirt is carved in a leaf-and-scroll design with floral garlands in the center of the long side, the scale is bolder than on laminated examples. The legs are double-scroll cabrioles with the stretchers crossing in scrolls to support an urn of flowers and leaves. An unusual detail of the stretchers is the motif of a rod piercing through on both sides. The size is right for a table in a library.

56. Table, writing or desk, walnut. H. 31½″, W. 56″, D. 31½″. Stenciled mark "Springmeyer Brothers, Successors to J. H. Belter." A rectangular tabletop form with two pedestals of storage space and a top drawer. Like a partners' desk in appearance, but the doors open on one side. There is rococo ornament in the brackets and on the doors.

57, 57a, 57b, 57c, & 57d. Bed, rosewood with laminated sides (17 layers of veneers). H. of head 75″, H. of foot 38½″, W. 66″, L. 80″. A four-part form following the suggestion and the shape in the patent. The undulating sides have carved decoration on each part. The headboard (57a) has flowers and scrolls, flanked by putti with a garland of leaves; the footboard (57b) is decorated with scrolls and a garland outside, and a lion's head (57c) within. The bed can be disassembled by lifting the upholstered centerpiece (57d) that covers the sidepieces.

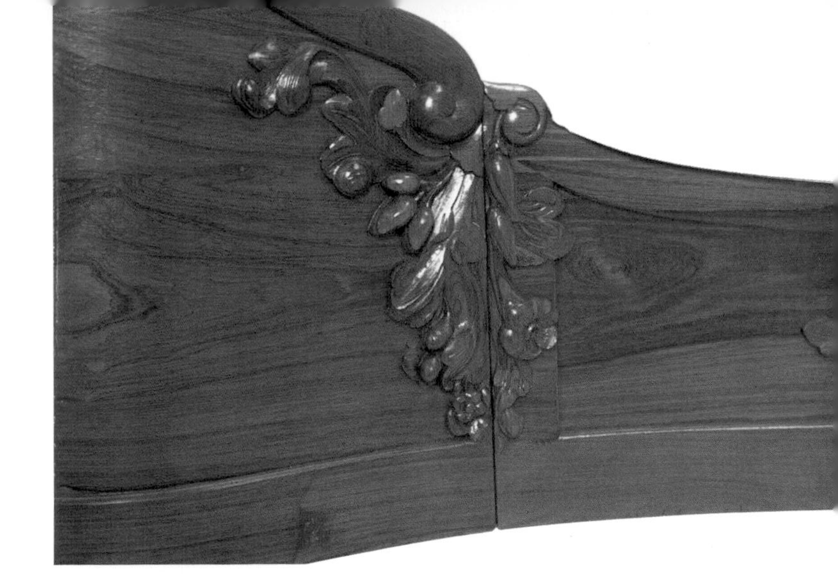

58, 58a, 58b, & 58c. Bed, rosewood with laminated sides (21 layers of veneers). H. of head 74″, H. of foot 38″, W. 66″, L. 80″. A four-part form with decoration on the headboard of birds (58a) before a cartouche-shaped scroll panel (58b), and the footboard has a simple floral cartouche (58c).

59 & 59a. Bed, rosewood with laminated sides (19 layers of veneers). H. of head 75″, H. of foot 37″, W. 66″, L. 80″. A four-part form with minimal decoration. "J. H. Belter, Patent Aug. 19, 1856" (59a) stamped on the rails.

61. Worktable, rosewood. H. 33″, W. 21½″, D. 17″. A rectangular box-shaped storage area with a sarcophaguslike cover and a lower drawer with tapering sides on simple cabriole legs supported by cross-stretchers that form a shelf in the center. There is pierced shell-and-leaf carving on the bottom drawer. This simple piece was used with a bed by Belter in a home furnished from the Belter shop.

62. Bed stand, rosewood. H. 27½″, W. 18″, D. 16″. A rectangular stand with a drawer and a door to close up the lower storage area. The drawer pull is in a grape and leaf design of molded sawdust composition. There is a cabochon on the door and scrolls at the front corners. Not by Belter.

60, 60a, 60b, 60c, 60d, & 60e. Bureau, rosewood with laminated details (4 layers of veneers on shelf; 10 layers of veneers on drawer front). H. 95¼″, W. 49″, D. 23½″. Four graduated drawers with undulating sides as illustrated in the 1860 patent (60a). The superstructure consists of an arched mirror framed with molding (60b). There are two shelves and a drawer on either side (60c). The piece is crowned with an elaborately carved crest of a basket of flowers centered on a floral and grape design. Pendant fruit and floral garlands embellish the corner columns (60d). The leafy scroll drawer pulls (60e) resemble the decoration of the tables at Rosalie.

BIBLIOGRAPHY

NINETEENTH-CENTURY REFERENCES

The Art Journal Illustrated Catalogue. The Industry of All Nations. London: George Virtue, 1851. Reprint. New York: Dover Publications, 1970.

DOWNING, A. J. *The Architecture of Country Houses.* New York: Appleton & Co., 1850. Reprint. New York: Dover Publications, 1969.

KIMBEL, WILHELM. *Journal für Möbelschreiner und Tapeziner.* Mainz, 1837–1839.

KING, THOMAS. *Designs for Carving and Gilding.* London: J. Weale, n.d.

SILLIMAN, BENJAMIN, and GOODRICH, CHARLES R. *The World of Science, Art and Industry, Illustrated from Examples in the New York Exhibition 1853–1854.* New York: G. P. Putnam & Co., 1854.

SMITH, GEORGE. *The Cabinet-Maker's and Upholsterer's Guide.* London: Jones & Co., 1828.

WHITAKER, HENRY. *The Practical Cabinet Maker and Upholsterer's Treasury of Designs.* London: Fisher, Son & Co., 1847.

KREISEL, HEINRICH. *Die Kunst des Deutschen Möbels.* 3 vols. Munich: C. H. Beck, 1968–1973. Third volume by Georg Himmelheber.

LICHTEN, FRANCES. *Decorative Arts of Victoria's Era.* New York: Charles Scribner's Sons, 1950.

ORMSBEE, THOMAS H. *Field Guide to Victorian Furniture.* Boston: Little, Brown, 1952.

OTTO, CELIA JACKSON. *American Furniture of the Nineteenth Century.* New York: The Viking Press, 1965.

STILLINGER, ELIZABETH. *The Antiques Guide to Decorative Arts in America 1600–1875.* New York: Dutton Paperbacks, 1973.

TRACY, BERRY, *et al. 19th-Century America: Furniture and Other Decorative Arts.* New York: The Metropolitan Museum of Art, 1970.

VINCENT, CLARE. "John Henry Belter Manufacturer of All Kinds of Furniture." Master's thesis, New York University, 1963.

ZWEIG, MARIANNE. *Zweites Rokoko.* Vienna: Anton Scroll & Co., 1924.

BOOKS

BISHOP, ROBERT, and COBLENTZ, PATRICIA. *The World of Antiques, Art, and Architecture in Victorian America.* New York: E. P. Dutton, 1979.

BUTLER, JOSEPH T. *American Antiques 1800–1900.* New York: The Odyssey Press, 1965.

COMSTOCK, HELEN. *American Furniture.* New York: The Viking Press, 1962.

DAVIDSON, MARSHALL. *The American Heritage History of American Antiques from the Revolution to the Civil War.* New York: American Heritage Publishing Co., 1969.

DOWNS, JOSEPH. *A Loan Exhibition of New York State Furniture.* New York: The Metropolitan Museum of Art, 1934.

DREPPERD, CARL. *Victorian, The Cinderella of Antiques.* New York: Doubleday & Co., 1950.

HIMMELHEBER, GEORG. Translated by Simon Jervis. *Biedermeier Furniture.* London: Faber & Faber, 1974.

PERIODICALS

DAVIS, FELICE. "Victorian Cabinetmakers in America." The Magazine *Antiques,* 44 (September 1943), pp. 111–115.

DOUGLAS, ED POLK. "Blessed Are the Meeks." *The New York-Pennsylvania Collector* (August 1979).

DOWNS, JOSEPH. "John Henry Belter and Company." The Magazine *Antiques,* 54, no. 3 (September 1948), pp. 166–168.

FOOTE, CAROLINE C. "A Victorian Cabinetmaker." *The Christian Science Monitor,* August 19, 1933, p. 5.

INGERMAN, ELIZABETH A. "Personal Experiences of an Old New York Cabinetmaker." The Magazine *Antiques,* 84 (November 1963), p. 576.

VINCENT, CLARE. "John Henry Belter: Manufacturer of All Kinds of Furniture." *Winterthur Conference Annual* (1973), pp. 206–234.

———. "John Henry Belter's Patent Parlour Furniture." *Furniture History* (1967), pp. 92–99.

INDEX

Page entries in **boldface** refer to illustrations.

One of the first graduates of the Winterthur Fellowship program, MARVIN D. SCHWARTZ, writer and lecturer, has worked in the field of nineteenth-century decorative arts for many years. His first encounter with Belter came in 1954 when he was Curator of Decorative Arts at The Brooklyn Museum. Among his publications are *American Interiors at The Brooklyn Museum* (1969), *Collector's Guide to Antique American Ceramics* (1969), *Collector's Guide to Antique American Glass* (1969), *Collector's Guide to Antique American Clocks* (1975), *Collector's Guide to Antique American Silver* (1975), *American Furniture of the Colonial Period* (1976), and with Betsy Wade, *The New York Times Book of Antiques* (1972).

EDWARD J. STANEK, Ph.D., is a graduate of St. Procopius College in Illinois and received his doctorate in physics from Iowa State University. He is the Director of Energy Policy for the State of Iowa and his avocation is writing and lecturing on antiques. He is the author of *Iowa's Magnificent County Courthouses* (1976) and *Antiques and Art Care and Restoration* (1978).

DOUGLAS K. TRUE was educated at the University of Iowa and received his master's degree in business administration from Drake University in Des Moines. He is the Deputy Director of Energy Policy for the State of Iowa.